KV-004-445

FLAME IN THE SNOW

FLAME IN THE SNOW

by
Veronica Black

Dales Large Print Books
Long Preston, North Yorkshire,
England.

British Library Cataloguing in Publication Data.

Black, Veronica
   Flame in the snow.

   A catalogue record for this book is
   available from the British Library

   ISBN 1-85389-669-1 pbk

First published in Great Britain by Robert Hale Ltd., 1980

Copyright © 1980 by Veronica Black

The right of Veronica Black to be identified as the author
of this work has been asserted by her in accordance with
the Copyright, Designs and Patents Act, 1988

Published in Large Print 1997 by arrangement with Robert
Hale Ltd.

All rights reserved. No part of this publication may be
reproduced, stored in a retrieval system, or transmitted in any
form or by any means, electronic, mechanical, photocopying,
recording or otherwise, without the prior permission of the
Copyright owner.

HAMPSHIRE COUNTY LIBRARY

1853896691

C013410890

Dales Large Print is an imprint of
Library Magna Books Ltd.
Printed and bound in Great Britain by
T.J. International Ltd., Cornwall, PL28 8RW.

FLAME IN THE SNOW

Kate Rye travels to Russia to meet her late father's relatives. In fashionable pre-revolutionary St Petersburg she meets her coldly dignified uncle, Count Narodny, and his sons Peter and Serge. On the way to Narodnia and in the great country house, real terror begins to stalk her. A mystery surrounds her father's death and her own birth, a mystery known to the crazy priest who seeks to warn her and to the one who plans her death...

ONE

The wind had flung lacy curtains of snow against the windows, obscuring the landscape. Kate, looking out, could discern only whirling whiteness pierced now and then by the yellow flare of storm-lanterns. February was a bitter month even in England but this was Russia and the cold had an almost tangible quality. She could practically taste it and when the train made an occasional stop to disgorge and swallow up passengers the opening door brought a blast of icy air that struck harshly against her face.

It was a pale face, long-nosed and wide-mouthed, redeemed from plainness by large brown eyes in the depths of which little points of amber sparkled. Her long hair, coiled into a heavy knot at the nape of her neck, was of the same light brown mingled with glints of gold.

Her travelling coat was of thick serge in a pattern of small green and grey checks, bordered at the cuffs and collar with grey

7

squirrel that matched her muff. A high crowned black hat was tied under her chin with a narrow green scarf and under the long skirt her feet were encased in high black boots.

'If you are determined to make this journey then you must dress suitably,' Miss Redvers had insisted. 'They say that in parts of Siberia one's blood actually freezes in one's veins unless one moves about constantly.'

Kate had stopped trying to explain that she was not going to Siberia, where she had a sudden mental vision of all the inhabitants running up and down to prevent their blood from freezing. The image thrown up by her mind curved her lips into a smile and the amber flecks in her eyes became laughing points of gold.

Miss Redvers, seated at her desk with the lawyer's letter before her, had shaken her head a little as she studied the tall, slim young woman opposite.

At twenty-one Katharine Rye had the makings of an excellent teacher. Discreet and intelligent, with a firm, pleasant manner that quelled the most rebellious pupils, she had worked at Redvers Court High School for nearly three years and given every cause for satisfaction. The headmistress, looking ahead to her retirement, had begun to hope she had found her successor. It was a pity that the girl's background was not more respectable. Miss Redvers had never believed the tale of a husband lost at sea and a posthumous baby that Mrs Rye had spun when she had first brought her eight-year-old daughter to the school but something in the child's still, waiting expression had softened her and she had agreed to take her at reduced fees on the understanding that she would later teach in the school.

Mrs Rye had been a well-educated woman herself, speaking vaguely of having spent a year as a governess in Russia. Miss Redvers had wondered about that but the small, fair-haired woman, lips primly folded, had never ventured any further information. She had died when Katharine was twenty-one.

'So it seems,' the headmistress said carefully, 'that your parents were never actually married. You must try not to dwell upon that, my dear. We are not to blame for our beginnings, and there are doubtless family reasons why they could not marry.'

"I am a bastard," Kate thought and knew that she had always suspected it.

'Your father was Russian,' Miss Redvers said, her voice tinged with the tolerance she reserved for foreigners.

'Boris Petrovich Narodny,' Kate nodded, quoting the letter.

'Who died six months before your birth.' The bit about the posthumous child had been true, Miss Redvers thought. Aloud she said, 'Your late mother felt it right that you should know about your background.'

But there had been nothing in the letter save the bare facts of Boris Petrovich Narodny's death, her own birth in England six months later and an address in St Petersburg. Kate had stared at that address, seeing in it both promise and challenge. She was not alone in the world, condemned to spend her days within the confines of a school. She had blood-kin, as yet unaware of her existence. A little gust of anger had shaken her, on her own behalf as much as her mother's. For years her mother had eked out an existence, living in cramped lodgings on the meagre income inherited from her own father, while the Narodnys sailed on in blissful ignorance of their English relative.

Within the week, not telling Miss Redvers, she had written to that address, heading it to the Family Narodny, telling whoever read her missive that she was the love-child of Boris Petrovich Narodny and Anne Rye. It was like throwing a stone into a deep pool. She wondered how far the ripple would spread.

The letter from St Petersburg had reached her a couple of weeks later. She had carried it to her room and sat for a long time, gazing at the delicate, slanting handwriting. She had not been sure whether to expect a reply or not and now that it was come she felt a sudden fear lest it disown her claim. She had not realised how deep ran her need to belong to a family of her own.

The letter was short but kind in tone. Her fingers trembled with relief as she held it. The writer had addressed her as 'my dear niece' and gone on to say,

'Your letter came as a surprise to me, but not a shock. Your dear mother was my governess many years ago, and though I was only a very young girl at the time I sensed that an affection was growing between her and my brother, Boris. His tragic death and her departure marked the end of my childhood, but I have often thought about her since. Word of her death grieves me but the grief is mitigated by knowledge of your own existence. We shall be most happy to welcome you here for a prolonged visit.'

A large cheque, payable from a London bank, and details of train times accompanied the letter and it was signed, 'Your affectionate aunt, Natalya Petrova Narodny.'

Kate had not expected such a generous and immediate response. Whatever reason Boris had had for not marrying her mother, his young sister had evidently had a sentimental regard for the lovers. Excitement quivered through her at the thought of meeting her relatives. Aunt Natalya had not indicated how many were in the family but she had used the pronoun 'we' and the size of the cheque hinted at wealth.

To her disappointment Miss Redvers had been less than enthusiastic when Kate had shown her the letter.

'Russia is a very long way away,' she had said doubtfully. 'A young lady cannot possibly travel so far without escort.'

'This is eighteen ninety-two,' Kate reminded her. 'There are trains and boats for me to take without the slightest danger to my reputation and St Petersburg is one of the most brilliant and civilised capitals in the world.'

'At least the letter is written in good English,' the other admitted.

'The whole family probably speak it fluently. French too. They are the languages of the upper classes in Russia.'

'You will require new garments against the cold,' Miss Redvers frowned.

'My aunt's gift will supply those and my travelling expenses,' Kate said eagerly, 'and there will be sufficient remaining for any incidental expenses.'

'I could grant you six months leave of absence,' Miss Redvers said slowly, 'but after that I could not guarantee to keep your position open. However the letter mentions a visit—'

'A prolonged visit,' Kate said. 'I believe I am to be made welcome among them for my father's sake. My mother's too. My aunt writes of her in most affectionate memory.'

'That's true.' The older woman's fingers drummed gently on the edge of the desk.

There was no denying that this was a wonderful opportunity for an orphaned young woman. Miss Redvers was fond of her protégée and the uncharacteristic dread that gripped her probably stemmed from her own selfish desire to keep an excellent teacher on her staff. Frowning, because nebulous fears were not part of her rational, modern outlook, she said, 'Then shall we say six months absence? You will require clothes and a passport and it may be possible for you to travel with a family.'

'You're very kind,' Kate said gratefully.

'As long as you don't expect too much from this visit. It was most reckless of you to write as you did,' Miss Redvers frowned.

'They are my kin. We have the right to meet.'

'As you say.' Miss Redvers refrained from pointing out that Anne Rye had kept her secret. She wondered why she had chosen to reveal it after her death. Perhaps she had hoped to provide her daughter with some insurance against penury. Again the obscure dread plucked at her and she said, more sharply than she had intended:

'Ought you not to be with your Junior French class?'

Kate had risen and gone out at once but teaching verbs to shiny-faced ten-year-olds lacked savour even at the best of times and her thoughts persistently returned to that welcoming but uninformative letter. Her mother had never spoken of Kate's father, never even mentioned his name. It was this extreme reticence, combined with a complete lack of photographs or personal mementoes, that had made the revelation of her illegitimacy less startling than it might have been.

The weeks following had flown by. There were travel documents and tickets to obtain, a letter to send giving the day of her arrival, clothes to buy on a whirlwind trip into the city. She had remembered her employer's advice and chosen warm garments but at the last, driven by that streak of recklessness that the headmistress deplored, had spent more than she intended on a low cut evening gown of pale lilac silk, its neckline edged with white swansdown, its long skirt drawn back into a small bustle. It was likely she would require such a gown in a fashionable household, she excused herself, and the dress flattered her slight curves, accentuating her narrow waist and

15

high breasts. The gown, together with her other purchases, reposed in the handsome leather portmanteau at her feet. She was cramped and stiff after days of travelling but the prospect of arrival made discomfort bearable.

'Colonel Metcalf's wife and daughter are travelling to Danzig, so you will be adequately chaperoned for most of the journey,' Miss Redvers had pronounced in relieved tones.

One of the Metcalf cousins was a pupil at the school, a fact which vouched for the unimpeachable respectability of the family. Miss Redvers wished she could have felt happier about the whole undertaking. She herself would have derived a mild, ladylike pleasure from such a trip but there was a streak of impulsive wildness in Katharine that leapt out occasionally from the carefully controlled young lady she had been disciplined to be. No doubt it was her Slavonic blood but Miss Redvers hoped that cool English sense would prevail.

'Now you will write to me, Katharine?' she had warned when they stood on the railway platform. 'Remember that your post will be retained for you until the autumn term.'

'Yes, of course.' Kate shook hands cordially and mounted the steps to the compartment with undisguised eagerness.

Mrs Metcalf, a seasoned traveller, as plump as her daughter, Amelia, was scrawny, proved an unexpectedly tactful companion, occasionally pointing out interesting landmarks but otherwise leaving Kate alone to think her own thoughts as the train chugged on the first stage of its journey.

The Channel crossing, although not excessively rough for the season, had prostrated both the Metcalfs, leaving Kate free to enjoy the unfamiliar sensation of pitching and tossing on a featureless grey sea, with the spray salting her lips and the wind catching the ends of her scarf and blowing it out over the high collar of her coat. As the train from Le Havre steamed through the misted meadows of Normandy towards Paris she had enjoyed her first French breakfast of croissants, runny apricot preserve and black coffee. Kate would have liked to spend a few days in the French capital but Mrs Metcalf was eager to rejoin her husband and they departed for Berlin after only an hour in the crowded station.

Travelling, Kate decided, gave one the strange feeling of being suspended between past and present in a perpetual now. Behind lay a dimly remembered childhood, schooldays at Redvers Court, the years of teaching in a familiar, almost cloistered environment. Ahead lay an unknown family, in an unknown country, who were at least disposed to welcome her. For the moment there was only the train, the changing landscape beyond the windows, the increasing cold as they turned northeast towards the Baltic and the borders of Poland.

'You will be certain to send me word that you arrived safely?' Mrs Metcalf requested as the train steamed into Danzig.

'Yes, indeed. I have your address.'

This was Russian territory or very nearly so, Kate thought. The quick-speaking Gallic French and the correctly formal German officials had given place to broader individuals as they examined her documents. The Metcalfs bustled away and she sat alone in her corner seat, her booted feet on her portmanteau, her eyes turned to the window against which the snow eddied and whirled.

Mrs Metcalf had evidently had a word

18

with the guard for at every stop he came along bringing mugs of steaming hot black tea and at midday two thin pancakes filled with sour cream and wrapped in a napkin.

'Blinis,' the guard said encouragingly, nodding at them.

She smiled back, bit into them cautiously and nodded approval. Her fellow travellers, muffled in furs and rugs, glanced at her with curiosity. Kate wished she could speak their tongue. As it was they probably regarded her as an eccentric foreigner.

It was difficult to realise that it was still only the middle of the afternoon for it was already as dark as midnight and the swaying oil lamps cast flickering shadows over the faces of the passengers. The train had slowed, no doubt for fear of ice on the track. Kate dozed a little and was jerked out of a half-dream by the grinding of brakes. For a moment she fancied they were at their destination but it was evidently a wayside halt. The door was opened and the ubiquitous guard appeared, beckoning her out onto the snow-covered platform. She clambered down with difficulty and was steadied by his muscular arm as the wind beat against her. There was a long wooden hut set back against the wall, its windows lit. Evidently it was a refreshment place of some kind for several of the other passengers were climbing down and making their way towards it. Kate was bustled to the doorway by the guard, who spread the fingers of both hands out, presumably to indicate a ten minute wait, and thrust her into a warm, smoke-filled room with a long counter running along one wall and a glowing stove in the centre.

The place was crowded, a few people having secured seats on the upturned barrels that served as stools, others standing at the counter or huddled around the stove. The strange tongue, that managed to sound both liquid and guttural at the same time, surged about her.

A huge copper vat behind the counter held what looked like thick stew. Kate dug out some coppers, holding them in the palm of one hand while with the other she pointed at the vat. Sign language evidently worked. The broad-cheeked woman with a kerchief over her hair, who stood behind the counter, took two of the coins, ladled soup into a mug and handed it to Kate with a piece of hard black bread, which evidently served as a spoon.

Kate, taking her example from those around, dipped in the bread and wedged into a corner, enjoying the peppery concoction. There was a lot of cabbage in the stew and some pungently spiced bits of meat in the rich brown stock. Some of her tiredness lifted from her and she looked about with interest, noting the kerchiefs and shawls of the older women, the high boots and furry caps of the men.

There was a sound beyond the windows that rose higher than the wind. The conversation faltered for a moment and then the high screaming came more clearly, mingled with the jangling of steel. The woman who had served out the soup crossed herself nervously and one of the men spoke a word under his breath that sounded like 'chort'.

The yelling ended in a high pitched whoop and she glimpsed the shape of horses and men beyond the snow-blurred window. Then the door crashed open and half a dozen men, booted and spurred, burst in.

She guessed at once who they were from the little she had managed to read about Russia since learning she was to travel here. Cossacks were the most brilliant horsemen and the most ruthless fighters in the vast Russian Empire. Bred on the steppes, descendants of the Tartars and mongols who had once ravaged the Middle East, they were both hated and respected by the ordinary citizen. Their loyalty to the Tzar was as much a legend as their savage cruelty if they were thwarted.

Kate stared at their broad faces and narrow eyes in fascination. One or two of them looked almost Chinese in cast of feature and texture of skin. The other customers had drawn back slightly creating a pathway for the newcomers. One taller than the rest and evidently their leader, to judge from the handsome wolfskin cloak that hung from his wide shoulders, slapped money onto the counter and the woman began to pour a clear liquid into the mugs, passing them to the men with quick, nervous gestures as if she feared hesitation might cause them to leap over the counter.

The tall man swung round, lifting his mug, calling 'Nazdorovye!' into the uneasy silence, draining the drink, slamming the mug down on the counter and motioning the woman to refill it.

He was young to be a leader, Kate

thought, probably less than thirty, but there was experience stamped on his features. His mouth and jaw were unyielding as granite below a jutting eagle nose and above the high, tanned cheekbones his eyes were narrow, slanting upwards, blue as aquamarines under locks of shaggy black hair that fell beneath his fur cap. He was not handsome save for those unexpectedly blue eyes but there was an elemental power in his face, a goatish grace in his thick torso and heavily muscled thighs that strained against the pleated cloth of his breeches.

The jewel eyes moved to her face and narrowed further as he arched one thick, black brow. Kate blinked rapidly, sliding her empty soup mug back on the counter, praying that he would turn his gaze elsewhere. There was some quality in his look that stripped her of her garments and made her feel naked in an alien world.

'*Nazdorovye?*' he said and to her embarrassed horror paced nearer, holding out the refilled mug.

Kate shook her head, forcing a tense little smile to her lips.

'Vodka,' the Cossack said. '*Nazdorovye.*'

'No.' She shook her head again, the smile pinned desperately to her mouth.

'*Nazdorovye!*' he repeated, thrusting the mug against her lips. Involuntarily they parted and fiery liquid splashed into her mouth. Spluttering, she jerked back her head, fear tightening into anger. The Cossack drank the vodka himself, tossing the empty mug to one of his companions who caught it, laughing. Then he stepped close again, so close that his breath fanned her cheek and his hands reached out, fastening on her shoulders, pulling her against him.

'I'm English. A British subject,' she heard herself gasp.

She was certain he understood. His eyes crinkled at the corners and his hard mouth twitched. For a long moment he stared at her and then he swept her into his arms, holding her bruisingly against him, and sank his teeth into her lip. Pain and shock robbed her of breath and for an instant she hung helplessly in his grasp. Then she tore herself free, wiping blood from her lip, spitting at him. The aquamarine eyes darkened to sapphire and fear of the consequences swept through her. The Cossacks were reputed to be a law unto themselves and if this barbarian chose to abduct her it might be weeks before enquiries were set afoot. Aunt Natalya would assume she had missed the train. Miss Redvers and Mrs Metcalf would imagine she was too busy to write. The thoughts chased through her mind as he stared at her and then he stepped back, hands on his hips, and deliberately, mockingly, burst into a roar of laughter. His men joined in, rocking to and fro, slapping the palms of their hands against their knees.

Kate's face flamed scarlet and the little points of amber in her eyes sharpened into daggers. One second longer and, Cossack or no Cossack, she would rake his cheek with her nails. Abruptly she turned and stumbled to the door, tugging it open against the wind, and, bending her head in a vain attempt to avoid the stinging snow, went towards the train. More by good fortune than good judgement she found the right compartment at once and hauled herself over the icy step, huddling into her seat with her fingers clenched achingly within her muff.

The other passengers were climbing aboard, giving her embarrassed little smiles as if they both deplored and admired her defiance. Through the open door she glimpsed the squat, fur-capped figures emerging from the refreshment hut and mounting their horses, who waited, snow-swept and patient. The tallest of them turned his head in her direction and she fancied that twin fires burned blue flame through the white curtain of snow. Then the door was slammed shut, hoarse voices shouted, the train shuddered and groaned forward.

Kate closed her eyes and leaned her head back, weariness flooding her again. Nobody, she thought with a glint of humour, would ever believe her if she told them what had happened. Not that she would ever dare to regale Miss Redvers with such a tale. In Miss Redvers's orderly world men did not stride into refreshments rooms and bite young ladies. Her lower lip still throbbed painfully. She put her finger to it gingerly and drew a deep breath. It had been the first time any man's mouth had touched hers and somewhere deep within her, beneath her anger, stirred a new and disturbing excitement.

She shivered, folding her hands within her muff again, and tried to fix her thoughts on what might lie ahead. The Narodnys were clearly rich and evidently prepared to welcome her. She wondered what her aunt looked like. There were no pictures of her father through which she might have made some comparison and she was too accustomed to her own face to seek for any foreign traits in its lineaments.

The wind had died from a howl to a murmur though the snow still fell steadily. The other passengers were beginning to gather together their bags and baggage. Some of them, nodding at her, said, 'St Petersburg.'

Kate struggled upright, smoothing down her skirt. The train was slowing and lights gleamed through the windows. In a few moments more they had shuddered to a halt and the bustle of a noisy station assailed her ears. Porters were coming down the length of the platform, wrenching open doors and calling the name of the station loudly.

A few minutes of confusion ensued while she continued to detain one of the porters for long enough to make him understand that she wanted herself and her portmanteau stowing into a cab. The driver peered at the address she had written on a piece of paper and shook his head, evidently unable to understand the roman characters.

'Narodny?' she said hopefully. St Petersburg was a large city and she doubted if one name would mean very much to him. For all she knew it might have been as common as Smith was in England.

'Count Narodny?' the coachman said. Count? She had no idea but the horses were stamping restively and she had to start somewhere.

'Count Narodny,' she said firmly and sat bolt upright as the carriage bowled into the street.

TWO

The drive was a short one through streets cleared by snowploughs but already icing over again. At each side lanterns made fairy-tale palaces out of high, balconied buildings. There seemed to be a constant procession of carriages passing up and down the wide thoroughfares and the jingling of bells sweetly pierced the air.

They turned into a small courtyard and

the coachman climbed down from his high perch and knocked at a side door. There were voices speaking Russian and then the carriage door was opened and a tall man in footman's livery stood at the side.

'You are Miss Rye, the lady expected?' His English was slow and heavily accented.

'Yes. Yes, I am.'

'Please to come. The ground is icy.' He leaned in and scooped her down, carrying her within the door and setting her carefully on her feet.

'I have luggage and I've not paid the coachman,' she began.

'That will be attended. Please to wait.' He vanished into the snowy yard, leaving her to take stock of her surroundings. She was in a large, square hall with a staircase curving sharply upwards. There were carvings of fruit and flowers on the white marble and thin brilliant rugs splashing colour over the floor.

'Mademoiselle?' A tall, thin woman in a black gown, her grey hair drawn back into a circled plait, was descending the stairs.

'I am Katharine Rye.'

'Je m'appelle Marisa.' Still speaking French the elderly woman continued. 'Your room is ready if you will follow me. Anton will bring up your cases.'

'I have only one,' Kate began but the woman was already mounting the staircase again and she had to hurry after her.

At the top of the second flight they crossed a hall similar to the one on the ground floor and Marisa ushered Kate into a large, luxuriously appointed bedroom decorated in shades of peach, warmed by a generous fire and furnished in what Kate believed was the style of the Second Empire.

'Your dressing-room is beyond.' The woman indicated another door. 'The Count has given orders that you are to be served supper here as he has an engagement to fulfil this evening. Here is Anton with your luggage. Do you wish me to unpack with you?'

'Thank you, no.' Kate watched the footman bring in her portmanteau, bow and withdraw. In his wake came a small servant-girl carrying a jug of hot water that looked much too heavy for her.

'Put the water into the basin. Mademoiselle requires to make her toilet,' Marisa ordered. 'Your supper will be brought in about half an hour.'

'My aunt—' Kate began.

'Madame Natalya is at Narodnia with Mademoiselle Anna,' Marisa said. 'I trust you have a comfortable night, Mademoiselle.'

Kate wanted to ask who the Count was and where Mademoiselle Anna fitted into the family but it would hardly do to begin questioning the servants. Marisa was evidently the housekeeper and obviously not as elderly as Kate had imagined. Under the crown of grey hair her face was youngish, her manner cool and stiff.

The water was hot, faintly scented. Kate removed her outer garments and washed herself with pleasure, enjoying the warmth against her chilled skin. There were fleecy towels in the dressing room and various jars of oils and powder. In the main bedroom the cupboards and wardrobe were empty. She unpacked, deciding that her new clothes looked worthy of their setting. At least she wouldn't disgrace these unknown relatives by appearing shabby.

A tap on the door announced another footman bearing a tray on which a cold supper was laid. He evidently spoke only Russian for he shook his head and spread his hands when Kate enquired when the Count would be home.

The supper was delicious. Cold roast duckling with a cherry preserve, asparagus tips, cheese-flavoured white bread and candied fruits tasted wonderful eaten in lamplight by a roaring fire. When she had finished she put the tray outside the door, hesitating as she wondered whether to explore. The tall house was silent and apparently deserted but she would feel a fool if Marisa caught her poking about. Instead she took some silky sheets of writing paper from an open case on the table and dashed off hasty notes to Miss Redvers and Mrs Metcalf informing them of her safe arrival.

Although it was not terribly late the fatigue of the long journey was overtaking her. Sealing the letters she undressed, lowered the lamps to a dull glimmer and climbed into the wide satin-hung bed. The last sound she heard was the plashing of snow against the curtained windows.

Bright sunlight and the swishing back of a curtain roused her and she struggled out of a deep sleep to blink at Marisa who had set a tray by the bed and moved to the window.

'Bonjour, Mademoiselle. Did you sleep well?'

'Very well, thank you. What time is it?'

'Ten o'clock.' Marisa consulted a fob watch pinned to her bodice.

'So late!' Kate sat bolt upright in dismay. At this time she had usually been teaching for an hour.

'Breakfast is served between nine-thirty and ten-thirty in the yellow room on the first floor. Will you take tea?'

Marisa had moved to the tray and was pouring from a Georgian silver pot.

'Thank you.' Kate accepted the cup of delicately fluted china. 'Is the Count at home?'

'He will be at breakfast,' Marisa informed her. 'Will you require the services of one of the maids?'

'No, I'm used to managing for myself,' Kate said.

'As you wish, Mademoiselle.' There was no change in the housekeeper's tone but Kate suspected that she had slipped a notch lower in her estimation.

Marisa went out silently. Kate drank her tea and dressed hastily. The long skirt of checked serge and simple green bodice, bought to complement the travelling outfit, looked reasonably fresh and uncrumpled. She coiled her straight brown hair into its usual knot and made her way down to the floor below. A long corridor led out of the hall and as she paused a door at the end opened and a dark young man emerged.

'You must be my English cousin,' he said, advancing with outstretched hand. 'I am most happy to welcome you to St Petersburg and regret very much that we were not here last night.'

He spoke fluent English though his manner was slightly flowery.

'Are you the Count?' she ventured, shaking hands.

'Me? Lord, no! I'm Peter,' he said.

'Peter.' She must have looked blank for he laughed, tucking her hand in his arm and escorting her into a sunny yellow-painted room.

'Father, this is Cousin Katharine,' he announced. 'Aunt Natalya evidently didn't explain the ramifications of the family when she wrote.'

The heavily-built man at the head of the table rose and bowed without extending his hand. He was in his forties but looked older, the black hair frosted, the grey eyes pouched in yellowish flesh.

'Mademoiselle Rye.' His voice and expression were equally cold.

34

'I am usually known as Kate,' she said with equal coldness. 'You must be—?'

'Count Alexis Petrovich Narodny,' the younger man said with a flourish. 'I am Peter Alexdrovich Narodny. Otherwise Uncle Alexis and Cousin Peter. Sit down and have some breakfast.'

He guided her to a chair and began to pile her plate with scrambled eggs and tiny sausages.

'We eat a hearty breakfast and make do with a light luncheon before the evening meal,' Peter said.

'My aunt—?'

'Hoped to be here to greet you but she seldom stays long in St Petersburg. My babushka is too frail to be left alone for very long and Anna cannot always cope.'

'My mother,' the Count said shortly by way of explanation. 'She is in her mid-seventies and not in good health. And Anna is my ward. Her parents were old friends of the family.'

'Anna is marked down as Serge's bride,' Peter said, 'when my dear elder brother can be persuaded to it.'

'Peter, I don't think Miss Kate is interested in our petty family squabbles,' Count Alexis said.

'But it's her family too,' Peter said. 'You know, cousin, your letter certainly set us all by the ears. We had no idea that a love-child had been born into our respected clan.'

'Peter, as you have finished your breakfast, we will excuse you,' his father said.

For an instant the glances of the two men met and locked. The younger was the first to drop his eyes.

'I will wait upon you later, cousin,' he said lightly and went out with a jauntiness that she guessed was assumed.

'You had better eat your breakfast before it gets cold,' the Count said.

Kate did as she was bade, aware as she ate that he was studying her closely. His coldly critical manner annoyed her but in the face of it she was determined to remain calm.

'I trust your journey was a comfortable one,' he said at last with an obvious attempt at politeness.

'Yes, thank you.' She answered with equal politeness, biting back the temptation to add, 'I was assaulted by a Cossack as a matter of fact, which added interest to the trip.'

'You look amused,' the Count said.

'Not really,' she said lightly. 'I was thinking I have come a long way for a scant welcome.'

'Do you expect me to feel proud of the revelation that my brother had an illegitimate child?' he demanded. 'We are an honourable family, Miss Kate, priding ourselves on our high standards of conduct. Your mother was employed as governess to my sister and ought to have been treated with respect.'

'I know none of the details,' she said hesitantly. 'As I said in my letter I was reared in the belief that my father had died at sea before my birth and that he and my mother were legally married. The information I received from the lawyers on my twenty-first birthday came as a complete shock.'

'Do you have that letter?' he asked.

She handed it to him silently and drank her cooling coffee.

'There is nothing here except the bare fact that you are the illegitimate daughter of Boris Petrovich Narodny,' he said.

'The address is there.'

'And on the strength of that you wrote to us?' He raised thick eyebrows and said, with nicely calculated insult, 'Even in

Russia, Miss Kate, bastards have no claim in law on any property. Even legitimate daughters receive only an eighth of any inheritance, the remainder being divided equally among the sons.'

So he took her for a fortune-hunter, an adventuress hoping for gain.

Her voice shaking a little, she said, 'My mother died four years ago and I have no other relatives. When I learned my father's name I naturally wrote. It was probably impulsive and ill-advised of me, and for that I apologise, but I was invited here—'

'By my sister, Natalya. She was your mother's pupil and devoted to both her and Boris. She wished to meet you and I agreed.'

'Unwillingly, it seems.'

'I am not as sentimental as Natalya,' he said dryly. 'You have, of course, no proof beyond this letter that you are Boris's daughter at all.'

'But I didn't come here to offer proof, only to visit my relatives,' she said stormily.

'You are indeed impulsive.' He gave her an unwilling smile. 'Well, since you are here, then we must contrive to make your visit as pleasant as possible. We return to Narodnia the day after tomorrow, to our country estate. The city seasons bores me and I make only a token appearance during it. Tonight there is a ball at the Winter Palace and tomorrow Kschessinska dances the Swan. You will wish to attend both events.'

She would have liked to inform him haughtily that there was absolutely no need for him to entertain her but the prospect of balls and ballet was an entrancing one and she said eagerly, 'I am well provided with clothes.'

'Thanks to Natalya's generosity,' he said coldly.

'She at least is disposed to welcome me,' Kate said, holding her own temper in check. 'So is your son.'

'Peter is a young fool where women are concerned. Even plain ones.'

She ignored the insult and enquired. 'You have another son?'

'Serge goes his own way,' he said briefly. 'In many families the eldest son is traditionally rebellious.'

She wanted to ask about her father but he was crumpling his napkin and rising from the table.

'The ball begins at eight-thirty, so be ready for eight,' he said. 'Marisa is skilled at dressing hair.'

It was probably another insult, she thought ruefully as he withdrew.

Peter came back as she was finishing her second cup of coffee. He was attractive, she decided, with his father's stern features softened into a gentler mould, his smile pleasant.

'Would you like to take a drive, cousin?' He leaned over her chair, his breath warm on her neck. 'It's stopped snowing and the sun has come out.'

'I'd love to take a drive.' She smiled back at him, grateful for his friendliness.

'Has my father been roasting you?' he enquired. 'Don't take it personally. He has a streak of morality running right through him. He always looked up to Boris.'

'Do you remember my father?' she asked.

'Hardly! I was born the year he died, but he's been held up to us as an example of masculine virtue for as long as I can remember. He's the uncanonised saint of the family. Now it seems he had a human weakness and father has to come to terms with it.'

'And your mother?'

'She died when I was a baby.' His face was sad for a moment and then brightened. 'Aunt Natalya reared us both, Serge and me, and there's Babushka.'

'Your grandmother?'

'Yours too,' he reminded her. 'She's very frail now and muddled in her mind, but she will welcome you, and Anna will be glad of a companion.'

'That's your father's ward.'

'Anna Nicholaevna Verotsky. Her parents died when she was a baby and she was brought up at Narodnia. She's seventeen now and not out yet, though it's time she was presented, but as she's to marry Serge there's no need for her to catch a beau.'

'You all have such long names,' Kate complained.

'It's simple really. We have our Christian name, then our father's name with "vich" or "ova" added, according to sex, and then the family name. Had you been born—pardon me—in wedlock then you would have been Katharina Borisova Narodny.'

'It sounds much grander than plain Kate Rye,' she said, amused.

'Go and get your coat and I'll show you the city,' he said.

They rode in a small, open carriage and her eyes sparkled as muffled in her garments she saw the great city flashing past. Her companion pointed out various sights, evidently bent on making her feel welcome.

'The whole city is built on a series of islands linked by bridges. That is the river Neva, but of course it's frozen now. Do you skate?'

'A little, but not much.'

'When we go to Narodnia we will go skating on the lake,' he promised.

'What's that spire?' she asked, pointing to the slender golden spear that pierced the sky.

'The fortress cathedral of St Peter and St Paul. You know that Peter the Great built this city two hundred years ago? He wanted Russia to become more Western in culture, so he looked towards Paris. This city is very French in feeling. Look, there is the Winter Palace. Did father invite you to the ball tonight?'

'He said I would be expected to go.'

'Very graciously phrased!' He slanted her a laughing look and said, 'Dear cousin, it will give me great pleasure to escort you. The balls are marvellous. I wish we could stay longer and attend more but father dislikes what he calls the dissipations of the city. We spend most of our time at Narodnia, but the St Petersburg house is much gayer. I believe my Uncle Boris liked it very much.'

'How did he die?' she asked abruptly.

'Uncle Boris? I don't believe I ever heard. There is the Cathedral of Our Lady of Kazan. Does it remind you of anything?'

'St Peter's Basilica in Rome,' she said promptly. 'I've seen pictures of it.'

'No wonder. It's a direct copy,' he said, as triumphantly as if he had built it himself. 'There is the Maryinski Theatre where the Imperial Ballet performs.'

'We are to go there too,' she said.

'Not me, my dear cousin. Serge is the balletomane,' he said. 'Father will escort you to that.'

'He said that someone called Kch— Ketch—?'

'Kschessinska. Mathilde Kschessinska. She is mistress to the Tzarevich, Nicholas. They say she is one of the most talented dancers in the Company, but I'm no judge of that.'

'The buildings are so pretty,' she said in wonder.

They soared upward, pinnacled, balconied and fretted with gold and copper, their walls painted delicate shades of pink, yellow, green and blue, with doors and window ledges picked out in white as gleaming as the sun-tipped snow piled up at the sides of the wide streets.

'It's the loveliest place in the world,' Peter said with enthusiasm. 'I promise you that Narodnia cannot hold a candle to it.'

'Will Narodnia be partly yours one day?' she enquired, hoping the question didn't sound too mercenary.

'No, thank the Lord. Under Russian law, when any daughters or widows have received their share, what remains is divided between the male heirs, so Serge will have Narodnia and I will have the St Petersburg house. We will divide it up amicably. I shall have what I consider the better part, though neither Serge nor my father would agree.'

'Will the Tzar be there at the ball?' she asked.

'Indeed he will! He's a fine figure of a man,' Peter said. 'Six feet four inches tall and as strong as a bull. The Tzarina Marie is very tiny, but they're happy together. She was a Danish princess before her marriage to him, but she has made herself completely Russian now and the people adore her.'

'And you?' She turned her head to look at him. 'Are you to be married?'

He shook his head. 'Not for years if I can avoid it. I want to have a good time first. The world is full of pretty women.'

And many of them would be happy to be escorted by such an elegant young man, Kate thought. She could appreciate his attractive qualities though her own pulse remained calm and steady. Perhaps she was a spinster by nature, she thought, and suddenly felt her cheeks flame hotly as the memory of the Cossack invaded her mind. The entire episode had been brief and shocking but for that moment as he crushed her to him she had felt fully alive, tingling with anger and excitement.

'I have kept you out too long in the cold!' Peter exclaimed. 'It takes time to become accustomed to the weather here. We'll drive back for a light lunch and then you will require time to get ready for this evening.'

Kate, who could be ready in an hour for one of the modest social events in the Redvers Court calendar, hid a smile. A ball at the Winter Palace was no doubt a very different affair.

Her uncle was nowhere to be seen and she and Peter lunched together in the yellow-painted room. There would be a tray brought up to her room at seven, he assured her, so that she would be fortified for the evening's dancing.

'Supper is never served until midnight at the Winter Palace and it's always a dreadful crush,' Peter explained. 'I don't know how many of the royal family will be there. The grand duchesses will probably be there and the Tzar's brothers, the grand dukes. They are formidable men, very powerful. I hope we manage to get a glimpse of them.'

'Will there be many there then?' she asked.

'About three thousand.' He grinned at her astonished look.

'Three thousand guests,' she echoed.

'Give or take half a dozen. Would you like another slice of tart?'

'Oh, no, thank you!' she said hastily, shielding her plate with her hand. 'People seem to do an awful lot of eating in Russia.'

'It keeps out the cold.' He stood as she pushed back her chair. 'Would you like to see the rest of the house now?'

At her assent he began to show her the main reception rooms, leading her through the handsomely appointed chambers as if he were employed as a guide in a stately home. It was a large house, built squarely on four floors. Peter confined his tour to the first floor where the yellow room, a dining-room, a library crammed with books, and two enormous drawing-rooms comprised the living space. He was an expert guide, she thought, as he displayed the various treasures scattered through the rooms.

'The vase belonged to the Empress Josephine once. My great-grandfather bought it after he visited Malmaison.'

'It's beautiful,' she said, bending to peer through the glass at the crystal set on a plinth of ruby velvet in a tall case.

'And these apostle spoons are very rare. They have tiny slivers of pearl set in the bowls so they shimmer when they catch the light.'

'You really do love this house, don't you?' she said, watching his intent look as he held one of the spoons up to the sunlight.

'Every nook and corner. When I was a little boy I used to long for the family to come to St Petersburg for the winter season. This house is beautiful and gay, not like Narodnia.'

His face was briefly shadowed and she impulsively laid her hand on his arm. He cheered up immediately, putting his own hand over hers as he exclaimed. 'But even Narodnia will be bearable now that you are come. I shall enjoy squiring you around, cousin.'

There was a slight cough from the open doorway and Marisa spoke in her precise French.

'If Mademoiselle wishes, her bath can be prepared now and we can discuss the hairstyle she intends to have.'

'I will see you later, cousin.'

Kate withdrew her hand, wondering if she had imagined the flash of alarm in the housekeeper's dark eyes.

The hip-bath in the dressing-room was half-filled with hot water and fresh towels had been laid out.

Kate luxuriated in the comfort of fragrantly scented water, washing the dust of the journey out of her long hair, splashing herself with the cooler water left in a jug at the side. When she had rubbed herself dry she sat by the fire to dry her hair, enjoying the quiet time that stretched between her and the ball. It was marvellous not to have to hurry over one's toilet for fear of being late for a class.

'Mademoiselle, I took the liberty of having the lilac dress pressed for you,' Marisa said, entering after the customary tap on the door. 'Do you require me to dress your hair?'

It was tempting to say that she could manage alone but she was anxious to look her best so nodded instead. Marisa was certainly skilled. She coaxed the long, straight mass of light brown into an elaborate coronet, working swiftly and silently. There was something in her manner that repelled conversation. Sentences rose to Kate's lips and died away unspoken and in the end gave up the attempt and sat mutely, watching a beautiful woman emerge from the chrysalis of plain Kate Rye.

THREE

The Count and Peter waited for her in the lower hall and she glimpsed unwilling admiration in the former's eyes as she came down the stairs. With her hair dressed high and decorated with tiny lilac bows to match the dress now partly concealed by a long cloak of black velvet, she both looked and felt quietly elegant.

A short drive through the lamplit streets brought them to the Winter Palace, its façade ablaze with lights, red carpet stretched across the pavement under an awning. Kate stepped from the carriage and on Peter's arm passed into an enormous white marble hall out of which a staircase, carpeted also in red, curved up to a wide gallery. A liveried footman took her cloak and she became part of a stream of brilliantly gowned women flowing up to the main ballrooms above.

In a blur of excitement she gazed around at the gold and white ceilings, the mirrored walls against which baskets of orchids and small palm trees were ranged, the tiny staircases winding to tiered seats from which one could gaze down at the throng of guests. She had never seen so many magnificent gowns or so much dazzling jewellery. Low-cut dresses of every possible shade, long trains bunched over apron-fronted bustles, lacy fichus and cuffs, ostrich feather fans, and all adorned with gems that caught the light from the huge chandeliers and flung it back in a thousand dancing rainbows. Her own lilac dress with its modest swansdown trimming was lost amidst all this grandeur and she was suddenly keenly aware of the fact that she possessed not a single jewel.

The galleried ballroom seemed to stretch for miles. Glancing at the marble floor Kate suspected that her feet would ache abominably before the evening was over. Against the wall at intervals troopers in white uniforms with breastplates and eagle-crested helmets of silver stood rigidly to attention. An orchestra was tuning up somewhere beyond the palms, and liveried servants were passing among the guests with silver trays bearing crystal glasses of red and white wine.

Peter took two glasses and handed

one to Kate. She gulped it a little too quickly and choked slightly. Her uncle had moved away and was greeting some other people, speaking French too swiftly for her untrained ear to follow. The prevailing language being spoken around her seemed to be French though she caught an occasional sentence in English and in what sounded like German.

There was a thin blare of trumpeters and the chattering voices were stilled. An official moved into the centre of the room, banging on the floor three times with his massive eagle-headed cane as he shouted, 'Their Imperial Majesties.'

The guests were shuffling into two ranks, the ladies rustling into deep curtsies, the men bowing. Sinking to one knee with the rest, Kate risked a brief upward glance at the huge, balding monarch in his bemedalled uniform. At his side walked the tiny dark-haired Tzarina Marie, glittering like some exotic bird in a silver gown sewn with diamonds, a diamond tiara on her small head. Behind them, in pastel-tinted lace embroidered with pearls and crystals, came two slender young women and a group of young men in full Court dress.

'The Grand Duke and Duchesses,' Peter murmured, assisting Kate to her feet. 'The dancing always begins with a polonaise. Will you partner me?'

She nodded eagerly, thanking her stars that Miss Redvers considered ballroom dancing a necessary part of a lady's education. This whirling mass of colour and light and music was however altogether different from the stiff-armed schoolgirls in their dark dresses whom Kate had partnered to the accompaniment of a tinkling piano.

At first sheer nervousness caused her to falter and lose the beat but Peter's arm steadied her and she began to enjoy the sensation of dipping and whirling, her dress a drift of lilac among the other gowns.

When the dance ended she was flushed and slightly breathless, her fingers tingling as she joined in the applause.

'Would you like another glass of wine?' Peter was enquiring.

'Lemonade, if there is any.' She allowed him to lead her to one of the small anterooms, shaded by tall palms from the main ballroom and furnished with gold framed chairs.

'Give me five minutes. The crowd will thin out later but there is always a mêlée at this stage of the evening.'

Peter escorted her to one of the chairs and hurried off.

Kate relaxed, spreading her skirts, tapping her foot in time to the music. She was actually here, at an Imperial Ball, dancing with an attractive and attentive cousin. It was something to be remembered and reported in as much detail as she could manage in her next letter to England.

A tall figure brushed past the shielding palm and a voice addressed her in a tone of amused surprise:

'*Stras vitye?*'

He was not in baggy breeches and wolfskin cloak this evening but in Court dress—or what she took to be Court dress—of tight elkskin breeches and high collared blue tunic belted in silver. His hair had been combed but there was no mistaking the narrow blue eyes so much at variance with the tanned skin and mongoloid features.

'One more step, you—barbarian, and I'll scream,' she began. 'I warn you!'

'*Kak dyelya?*' he returned, taking the threatened step.

54

'I don't speak your language.' Her voice rose in panic. The palm leaves rustled again as Peter, to her unspeakable relief, came back with the lemonade. His eyes, falling on the Cossack, expressed surprise. 'Serge! What the devil are you doing in St Petersburg? I thought you were trapping at Archangel!'

'Changed my mind,' the other said in perfect English. 'Anyway I wanted to take a look at our English cousin. I presume this is she?'

'Cousin, may I present my elder brother, Serge Alexdrovich Narodny, and apologise for his blunt speaking. Serge, this is Cousin Katharine Rye who prefers to be known as Kate,' Peter said.

'Leave me to do my own apologising and take my place in the set, there's a good fellow,' Serge said, clapping his brother on the shoulder and twitching the glass of lemonade out of his hand. 'Your refreshment, cousin. We will sit here and get acquainted while you disport yourself in the quadrille.'

'If you'll excuse me then?' Peter bowed and went back to the dancing.

'Pretty-mannered lad, isn't he?' Serge observed, looking after him.

'You ought to have told me,' she began faintly.

'Dear Katinka—may I call you Katinka?' He sat down on the other chair which creaked slightly under his weight.

'My friends call me Kate,' she said frostily.

'Ah, but we cannot tell on such short acquaintance whether we will be friends or not,' he said provokingly, 'so I shall call you Katinka. I promise you I had no idea who you were when I met you yesterday.'

'You make a habit of insulting young ladies, do you?' she enquired, sipping her lemonade.

'In Russia young ladies don't usually travel unescorted,' he said blandly.

'It was insufferable conduct,' she said.

'Ah, I fear my friends and I had already made an evening of it.' His hard mouth twitched.

'Friends!'

'Very loyal ones. I hold an honorary commission in the Cossack Life Guards. My great-grandmother was a Cossack woman, though the rest of my family prefer to talk about the other great-grandmother who was Swedish and brought the blue eyes into our blood line. So you are Uncle Boris's by-blow?'

'If you must put it that way.'

'You would prefer to call yourself a love-child, I suppose.' He raised a mocking eyebrow and she flushed angrily, bending her head over the clouded liquid in her glass.

'For my own part I was rather happy to learn that our late lamented uncle was not quite the saint that family tradition has made him,' he said.

'Do you remember him?'

'I've a vague picture in my mind but I suspect that it's based more on what Aunt Natalya has told me than on personal recollection. I was only a small boy when he was killed.'

'Killed!' Kate jumped slightly and the ice in her glass tinkled sharply.

'A skating accident. There was a thin patch of ice in the middle of the lake where he went through. I've only the vaguest memory of it and it's confused with my mother's death and Peter's birth. That was an eventful year.'

His tone was sombre and the teasing glint had vanished from his eyes. It returned as he lifted his head and said, 'So you are my cousin? What did you hope to gain from your visit, I wonder? I don't suppose you have a sweetheart, so we must throw you into the path of a Grand Duke or someone of that ilk!'

'Very kind of you,' she snapped, 'but I've no intention of being thrown anywhere! I'll choose my own husband if and when I decide to take one.'

'But at twenty-one,' he said, 'you must take care you're not left on the shelf.'

Her face flamed again but she bit back a retort, determined not to rise to the bait.

'My father was not overjoyed to hear of your existence,' he continued. 'He dislikes scandal.'

'I don't intend to cause any,' Kate said tightly.

'Your very presence will give rise to gossip in polite circles. Aunt Natalya is too unworldly and sentimental to appreciate how vicious tongues can be. Society in St Petersburg is riddled with hypocrisy.'

'I think it's a beautiful city,' she said defiantly.

'As pretty as icing on a cake,' he nodded. 'I'll tell you something, cousin. This Winter Palace is the Versailles of Russia and nobody hears the passing bell because the music of the waltz is too loud. One day these perfumed aristocrats will be swept away and the cold wind of reality will howl through these walls.'

Kate found herself shivering as if she already felt the cold wind. His voice no longer teased and tormented her but was low and intense and his eyes stared past her as if he gazed into a future she couldn't envisage.

'We travel to Narodnia the day after tomorrow,' she ventured, wanting suddenly to shake him out of his mood. 'Peter says that he prefers the city, but he will be coming with us.'

'Will he indeed!' Serge's attention snapped back to her. 'You must have made a decided impact on him. My brother usually has to be dragged screaming out of balls and dinner parties.'

'I like him very much,' she said.

'I am particularly fond of him myself,' he said. 'Indeed I am far too fond of him to stand by idly while he falls into the clutches of a fortune-hunter.'

This was too much to endure. A thin white line appeared around her mouth and her eyes flashed golden sparks as she rose, holding her head high.

'My uncle is of the same opinion,' she said, her voice shaking with anger. 'I shall take great pleasure in disabusing both of you of that! Excuse me, please.'

'Oh, but you cannot possibly wander about alone,' he said at once, rising with her.

'I cannot imagine that I could possibly be subjected to more rudeness than I have received so far,' she retorted.

'Then you must forgive my boorish ways,' he said, looking quite unrepentant. 'I may be mistaken in my judgement, in which case I shall apologise handsomely and bid you welcome for your father's sake.'

'My father never saw fit to wed my mother despite his saintly reputation,' she said. 'If you bid me welcome, let it be on my own account, and don't bother with apologies.'

'You've spirit!' he exclaimed and broke off as the Count came in.

Uncle Alexis looked as grimly disillusioned as ever and the gaze he directed at his heir was sardonic.

'Peter told me that you were here. It isn't often you grace the fleshpots of the city,' he observed.

'I was eager to meet my English cousin. She is really quite charming,' Serge said equably.

'Are you enjoying yourself, Miss Kate?' the older man asked.

'It's so grand that it's a little over-whelming,' she confessed.

'Tomorrow we go to the ballet. Will you join us there?'

'With pleasure, father, but I'll lodge in town. You know how stifled I feel in that museum of a house.'

'I know you seldom take a step without breaking something,' his father said dryly. 'I must pay my respects to the Rostoffs, Miss Kate.'

'Uncle Alexis.' She stressed the first word slightly.

He and Serge might only tolerate her existence but she was their blood kin and not prepared to allow them to forget the fact.

'I owe you thanks,' Serge said as his father went out. 'You might have complained of my rude conduct last night.'

'I was taught that it was wrong to tell tales,' she said.

'Ah, there speaks the correct English

schoolteacher, standing there so primly with that lemonade glass held like a gun between your hands.'

Before she could answer he had plucked it away, set it down and pulled her into his arms. She heard herself make one strangled squeak of protest and then his own lips pressed down upon hers, his tongue flicking between them, and her lower limbs were turned to water so that she had to clutch at him to keep her balance.

'And that,' he said, raising his head and looking down at her, 'is the second time I've kissed you in twenty-four hours.'

'And I enjoyed it even less the second time!' she exclaimed furiously, struggling free and wiping the back of her hand across her mouth.

'I enjoyed it more,' he said, looking amused. 'There is a yielding softness in you that contrasts with your prickly exterior, Katinka.'

'Kate,' she said between her teeth. 'My name is *Kate!*'

He was chuckling in a manner that infuriated her still further. Kate swung about on her heel and went back into the great ballroom again, snapping open the lilac fan that hung from a ribbon at her waist and using it vigorously to cool her hot cheeks.

'There you are, cousin!'

She turned in relief as Peter came up to her, his smile frank and pleasant in welcome contrast to his brother's mocking grin.

'They are dancing the mazurka next and then the chaconne. Will you risk a mazurka with me?'

'Willingly, though I'm not certain of all the steps,' she said promptly.

'Has Serge deserted you?' he enquired, taking her arm.

'It is more a matter of my deserting him,' she said. 'He seemed to share your father's opinion of me as someone who seeks only to make trouble in the family.'

'You mustn't mind Serge,' Peter consoled. 'His bark is much worse than his bite, I assure you. He is one of the best fellows in the world when you get to know him.'

Kate was not in the least sure she desired any further knowledge of Serge but Peter evidently admired his elder brother so she let the matter drop and concentrated her attention on the mazurka, congratulating herself silently when the dance drew to its close without her making too many mistakes.

The chaconne followed and then a series of rapid waltzes which left her breathless with the aching feet she had dreaded earlier.

'Shall we have supper?' Peter enquired.

She assented gratefully and they moved into an adjacent chamber, the first of many leading one from another and crammed with small tables on which a variety of food was temptingly arrayed. Kate had not expected to be hungry, but the eggs stuffed with caviar, the chicken mousses, the colourful jellies and salads, the dressed lobster and pastry tartlets with the swirls of whipped cream made her mouth water.

'Will Serge be joining us?' she asked and wondered why she had bothered to enquire, for his whereabouts were of no interest to her.

'He never stays very long at these affairs,' Peter told her, passing cold sturgeon decorated with stuffed olives and tiny radishes sliced into roses.

'Oh,' she shrugged and tasted her supper.

'He's a good fellow,' Peter said again, looking embarrassed. 'You must try to understand him. He's not many years older than we are but he has different ideas about Russia being Russian and not a modern European country.'

'He probably takes after your Cossack great-grandmother,' she said waspishly.

'Did he tell you about her?' Peter laughed, leaning to pour champagne. 'She was a terrible woman, from all accounts. Rode astride like a man, cracking a whip about her head. Babushka was her daughter but Babushka is gentle.'

'I look forward to meeting her.' Kate put Serge firmly out of her mind.

'Of course, she's your grandmother too,' he said, raising his glass to her. 'She never learned to speak more than a few words of English, I'm afraid, but if we can impress on her who you are then she'll be pleased. She's a very tolerant woman.'

Kate was not certain she welcomed the idea of being tolerated but she raised her own glass in reply.

'*Nazdorovye!* Good health!' Peter said.

The champagne was thin and cold, fizzing against her nose. The vodka that splashed into her mouth had burned and left a mellow warmth. She drank the champagne and smiled.

'The Tzar comes this way,' he said in a low voice. 'Go on with your supper as if you had noticed nothing. He likes informality.'

It was an odd kind of informality, Kate thought, peering at the huge figure with his entourage moving between the tables, pausing now and then to boom out a greeting.

'He's not coming to this table,' Peter said, his voice disappointed. 'I hoped you might have been presented.'

'I'm glad that I was not,' she said frankly. 'I am not grand enough.'

'Cousin, you look charming,' he said. 'Elegant simplicity will be next year's style.'

'Well, it certainly isn't this year's,' she said dryly, glancing about her at the elaborately draped bustles and sparkling jewels.

'Come to the window,' he invited. 'All the windows on this side overlook the river. It's frozen now, of course, but the lights make beautiful patterns on the ice.'

They moved to one of the huge windows and looked down through double sheets of glass onto the shining expanse of shifting rainbow colours that were reflected in the dark sky above.

'My father died when he was skating, didn't he?' she said abruptly.

'Who told you that?' His voice was kind and concerned.

'I asked Serge. You told me that you didn't know.'

'I didn't want to upset you,' he said. 'It was a very long time ago and I only know what I was told. There was a thin patch on the ice and Uncle Boris went through it and was drowned. They found his body when the spring thaw came, caught in the rushes at the end of the lake. It must have drifted there. Aunt Natalya told us about it when we were older. It was a terrible accident.'

'Serge told me that in the same year your mother died?'

'A few months after I was born. She was a delicate woman and she caught a chill and died of it. These are gloomy thoughts for a ball!'

'I want to know about the family, the good and the bad,' Kate said eagerly.

'Oh, we are not a very large or exciting lot,' he said. 'Babushka lives in retirement with Aunt Natalya to look after her and

Anna Nicholaevna to help her. Aunt Natalya wishes Anna to marry Serge but Serge refuses to agree.'

'Does Anna want to marry your brother?' she asked curiously.

'She is my father's ward,' Peter said, as if no further answer were needed.

'Your father never married again?' she said.

'He and my mother were wed when both were seventeen,' he said. 'My mother died four years later and my father swore then he would never take another wife. He is happy in the country. You don't see him at his best in the city. That is something he and Serge have in common.'

'But he won't marry to please your father.' An unwilling respect stirred in her for Serge's independent outlook.

'Serge is rebellious,' Peter said, rather as if he were commenting on his elder brother's choice of suit. 'You really will like him very much when you get to know him better.'

Kate had no intention of getting to know Serge at all but she smiled vaguely, her eyes fixed on the gleaming ice below the window.

'Father will be waiting for us,' Peter

said. 'He never stays at these events for very long either.'

Kate felt as if she had been there for ever. The champagne and the rich supper had combined to give her a severe headache and her feet were burning.

'Come then.' Peter offered his arm and they made their way slowly back to the main rooms where a few couples were still dancing to the strains of the orchestra while others were making their leisurely way down the magnificent staircase to the hall, where the servants were waiting with cloaks and wraps. Kate wondered how on earth they matched owners up to garments but her own black velvet cloak was soon around her shoulders.

'Did you enjoy your supper?' the Count enquired, helping her up into the carriage.

'Very much,' she said.

Serge had not asked her to dance. She wondered if he danced as gracefully as so many heavily built men did.

'These affairs are all pomp and vanity,' he said sourly. 'Olga, my wife, used to enjoy them very much and I took pleasure in her pleasure but now they bore me.'

'You like Narodnia better,' she said.

'Narodnia is the family home,' he said

69

flatly. 'Serge and Anna will be master and mistress there one day.'

'While I fly the family flag in St Petersburg,' Peter said cheerfully. 'Father, Serge said he was accompanying you both to the ballet tomorrow.'

'I may decide to indulge myself with a quiet evening at home,' his father said. 'You will not object if Serge escorts you, Miss Kate?'

'No, of course not.' She took a deep breath and coughed as stray flakes of snow swirled into her mouth. They had reached the Narodny house and Anton appeared to help her over the icy step.

'Will you have a glass of tea?' Peter enquired as they started up the stairs. 'Father and I usually have a brandy and soda and mull over the day's events.'

'I think I'll go straight to bed if you don't mind. Thank you for the evening,' she said.

'It was a pleasure,' Peter began but her uncle cut across him quellingly.

'As my brother's daughter and a stranger to the city, you are naturally entitled to be treated with a certain hospitality. There is no reason why your visit shouldn't be a pleasant one.'

'Then I wish you would call me Kate,' she said impulsively. ' "Miss" sounds so formal, as if I were still teaching in school!'

'Good-night then, Kate.' He pronounced the name with an obvious effort.

'Good-night, Uncle Alexis. Cousin Peter,' she answered pleasantly, pleased by her small victory, and went up to her room.

FOUR

She slept late the next day, waking at noon with her headache gone and her feet only slightly burning. Marisa was evidently occupied elsewhere for the little maid who spoke only Russian came up with hot water and a tray on which tea and hot pancakes nestling in a napkin were arranged.

The house was silent but the noises of the city drifted through the windows and when she looked out she could see fur-capped children below throwing snowballs and shrieking with laughter. When she had dressed she went down to the lower rooms with the intention of getting a book from the library. As she entered the shelved apartment with its fittings of coral and black walnut the Count looked up from a large, flat-topped desk inlaid with ivory.

'Good-morning.' He gave her a crisp nod and what passed for a smile.

'I'm sorry I missed breakfast,' she began.

'No need. Peter went out to make his farewells to various acquaintances. We start out early tomorrow, so I would advise you to come back straight after the ballet tonight and not go on to supper anywhere afterwards.'

'Perhaps I ought not to go.'

'Nonsense, you mustn't miss the chance of seeing Kschessinska. She is a most promising performer if she doesn't allow her position as the Tzarevich's mistress to go to her head.'

'Do we go by train to Narodnia?' she asked.

'The line doesn't go in that direction. We live nearly a hundred miles north of the city, so in winter we travel by troika or ride. It's a two-day journey but we break it at the Monastery of St Serguis for the night. They provide for travellers.'

'And this house is shut up?'

'Except for the servants. Peter usually

comes here for a couple of months in the summer but I prefer Narodnia.'

'Will Serge be travelling with us?' she asked casually.

'Serge makes his own arrangements,' her uncle said. 'He is not answerable to anybody and I refuse to play the tyrant father.'

Kate hesitated, then said abruptly, 'You have not told me anything of my own father. I would really like to know.'

'He was a very fine young man,' Count Alexis said slowly. 'He was a year my senior but quiet and gentle, a bookish young man. Our father thought at one time that he might have a calling to the priesthood.'

'And you didn't know that he and my mother—?'

'Your mother was employed as governess,' he said. 'Natalya was only sixteen and about to make her debut in society and my father decided that she required her knowledge of English polishing. I was already married and Peter was on the way, so it's possible my attention was taken up with my own affairs, but I am certain nobody dreamed of any—affection between Boris and your mother.'

'Did you like my mother?' she asked bluntly.

'I scarcely knew her. Olga and I spent the early years of our marriage in St Petersburg but my father wished his second grandchild to be born at Narodnia, so we moved back there for Peter's birth. A few months later my brother lost his life in that unfortunate accident and a few days later Olga died. She was not a strong woman and I fear the shock, coming so soon after her recent confinement, proved too much for her.'

'And my mother?'

'She left. I remember my father was annoyed at her lack of consideration. I'm afraid I was too preoccupied with my own grief to have time for the comings and goings of a governess.'

'I wondered if I was like my father,' she ventured.

'You have his nose and the same hair colouring,' he said unwillingly, 'but I see nothing else of him in you.'

"Or don't want to see it," Kate thought with irritation, "because you don't want your saintly brother to fall off his pedestal."

'Your aunt will be able to see a resemblance,' he continued. 'Natalya is a sentimental woman and your letter threw her into a great state of excitement. She sees you as a long-lost niece, a proof that Boris left something of himself behind.'

It was plain from the sarcasm of his voice that he didn't share his sister's view. Kate ignored the sarcasm and went over to the shelves to choose a book. There were several English titles there and she took out a volume of Fanny Burney. Spicy Regency gossip would take her mind off the questions that still teased her.

'The performance begins at nine so dinner will be at seven,' the Count said, bent over his papers again.

'Thank you.' She hesitated, wondering if he would volunteer any further information about her father but he was adding up columns of figures and took no notice of her.

Miss Burney's wit had little power to distract her. Kate turned the pages idly without taking in the sense of the words. Twenty-two years before, a gentle young man had gone out skating and fallen through the ice, to drift into the rushes and be held there until the spring thaw. And by the time the ice melted Olga, the wife of his younger brother, had been in her grave for months and the governess had returned to England to bear her child. Kate wondered why her mother had never returned to Russia, never asked the Narodnys for help. Above all she wondered why the identity of her father should have been revealed to her when she was twenty-one. Surely her mother had guessed she would seek out her Russian relatives.

Lunch was a silent meal. The Count apologised briefly for his haste, saying he had an appointment and hurrying away after the first course. Peter didn't put in an appearance at all and Kate finished her meal alone with only Anton hovering in the background.

When she went up to her room again Marisa was there, laying the lilac dress over the foot of the bed.

'I took the liberty of having your gown freshened, Mademoiselle,' she said, straightening up. 'Will you require me to dress your hair?'

'If it's no trouble,' Kate said.

'Mademoiselle Natalya gave instructions that you were to be made comfortable,' Marisa said.

'I take it that you've been with the family for a long time,' Kate said, detaining her.

'I entered the service of the Narodnys when I was ten,' Marisa said. 'I was allowed to share Mademoiselle Natalya's French and English lessons.'

'Then you knew my mother!'

'Yes, Mademoiselle. I knew her.'

'Yet you speak only French,' Kate remarked.

'I have always found English an ugly language,' Marisa said.

There was a subtle insult in her tone which Kate chose to ignore.

Instead she said, in a voice which she contrived to make both firm and pleasant:

'You have made me very comfortable, Marisa. I shall make a point of telling my aunt about it.'

'You are coming to Narodnia then?'

'We travel tomorrow, don't we?' Kate said lightly.

'It is a long journey,' Marisa said.

'Two days. I look forward to it,' Kate said.

'As Mademoiselle wishes.' The housekeeper seemed about to say something else but evidently thought better of it and, excusing herself, withdrew silently.

When she returned later she was in an uncommunicative mood, failing to respond to any of Kate's remarks as she dressed her hair in a high coronet and helped her into the lilac gown. The only remark she volunteered was the sly, 'In St Petersburg the ladies are noted for their jewels.'

'I saw some of them last night,' refusing to be drawn.

She wished privately that she had even a simple necklace to cover the bareness of her throat but she would not have admitted as much to the woman who so obviously disliked her and made it clear that she served her only because Mademoiselle Natalya had ordered her to do so.

Dinner had been set for three in the crystal-hung dining-room. Kate drew a deep breath as she went in, having caught a glimpse of Serge's broad shoulders through the half-open door.

'Good evening, my dear cousin.' He rose as she came in, pulling out her chair for her. 'I am here as promised, you see.'

'It's very good of you to take the trouble,' she said without expression.

'Nonsense! I am always delighted to escort a personable young lady,' he returned blandly.

'And you have the good sense to enjoy

the ballet,' his father put in.

'That surprises me,' Kate said. 'I would not have imagined that the ballet appealed to you at all.'

'But you don't know me very well, cousin.' The brilliant blue eyes narrowed at her in silent, mocking amusement.

"Nor do I wish to," she thought and drank her soup demurely while the two men chatted in a desultory manner about various people whose names were unfamiliar to her. As the lemon soufflé was being handed Serge fixed his attention upon her again, saying:

'So tomorrow you go to Narodnia?'

'I look forward to it,' she said with a little touch of defiance.

'Aunt Natalya will welcome you,' he said.

Implicit in the remark was the sentiment that Aunt Natalya's opinions were not taken very seriously by the rest of the family. Kate ignored the implication, fixing a sweet smile to her lips as she said:

'It will be wonderful to meet her. I understand my grandmother will be happy to meet me too.'

'Your grand—oh, Babushka.' He looked slightly nonplussed as if he had not really considered the fact that they shared the same grandmother.

'My mother is old and lives very much retired,' the Count said. 'It's very possible that she may not realise exactly who you are. Will you have coffee, Serge, or ought you to be leaving?'

'We ought to be leaving, if we're not to miss the overture,' Serge said promptly. 'I'm sorry you're not coming, Father.'

'I have the accounts to finish. Your cousin's arrival disordered the routine,' the Count said.

Kate gave him an indignant stare. She had never met people who made her feel so unwelcome while contriving to observe the social niceties.

'Shall we go then, cousin?' Serge was on his feet and she rose, ignoring his proffered arm and sweeping through to the hall where Anton stepped forward with her cloak.

They rode in silence to the theatre, Kate being determined not to expose herself to more insult, Serge being apparently wrapped in his own thoughts.

When they entered the blue and gold foyer, however, she couldn't repress a cry of delight. Crystal chandeliers illuminated the bejewelled women who crowded the wide space, calling greetings to their friends, smiling up at their escorts. Music drifted down the wide staircase from an unseen orchestra above and the air was heavy with perfume.

'It is beautiful,' she said defensively.

'Very beautiful,' he agreed, slanting her a smile. 'We'll take our seats, shall we?'

She had expected a seat in the dress circle, where she had once spent an enchanted evening when her mother had taken her for a birthday treat to the theatre in London. At the top of the stairs, however, they turned into a wide corridor with doors set in it at intervals. Serge pushed one of these and she entered a bow-fronted box hung with blue and gold curtains.

'We keep a permanent box here during the winter season,' Serge said.

'One can see the entire theatre from here,' Kate said.

'For my own part I come to watch the dancing,' he said, 'but most ladies like to evaluate the competition, making eyes at prospective lovers.'

'You don't have a very high opinion of women, do you?' she challenged.

'That depends on the woman. I count breeding as important.'

'And you don't consider it good breeding for anyone to make her existence known to a family ignorant of it?'

'I couldn't have phrased it more neatly myself.'

'Nor made it more clear that you resent my coming. Why? Don't I have the right to meet my blood kin?'

'You might have caused great harm,' he said. 'As it is we all have to come to terms with the fact that my Uncle Boris, the nearest to a saint the Narodnys have ever produced, actually had a sordid liaison with an English governess and sired a daughter.'

'How ready you are to call it "sordid",' she exclaimed. 'Perhaps they truly loved each other, or are you incapable of understanding that?'

'Oh, I'm constantly in and out of love,' he said, helping her off with her cloak.

'Then you don't understand it,' she said flatly. 'I wanted to meet my father's people. Is that so wrong?'

'Did you never stop to think, before you wrote to us, that you might be dropping a bombshell into the midst of a family that prides itself on its bloodline?'

'There's nothing wrong with my blood-line,' Kate said with a quiet fury. 'My mother was a lady and whatever happened between her and my father I can tell you one thing. She was a gentlewoman, who worked hard all her life to bring me up decently.'

'I intended her no insult,' he said with surprising mildness. 'But you must admit it was grossly impulsive of you to write announcing your existence. You couldn't have known how the news would be received. Suppose my grandfather had still been alive! I tell you that he would have had an apoplectic fit.'

There was a certain truth in what he said, for she had written on impulse without considering the effect her news would have upon the family, but at that moment she would have died rather than admitted it. Her face flaming, she said:

'Are we here to watch the ballet or to listen to your lecture?'

'Let us watch the ballet by all means,' he returned. 'I'd not have you miss the best part of St Petersburg.'

There was a stir in the audience and

a rustling as seats were tipped back and they rose.

'The Tzarevich is here,' Serge said, rising too.

'Where?' Kate was on her feet, craning her neck. Most people in the audience seemed to be doing the same.

Serge nodded towards a box opposite, where a slender, dark-haired young man was taking his seat. There was a smattering of applause and more rustling as the audience resumed its seats.

'Has he come to see his—friend?' Kate whispered.

'His mistress,' Serge corrected, a gleam in his eye. 'Kschessinska is a lovely girl. The affair will come to nothing, of course. The Tzarevich Nicholas is intended to marry Princess Alix of Hesse if she can be persuaded to change her religion from Lutheran to Greek Orthodox.'

'And the dancer?' she questioned.

'She will receive a handsome pension,' Serge said. 'One could scarcely have a ballet dancer as future Tzarina of all the Russias.'

There was something chilling in his indifference. Kate cast a sympathetic look towards the slight, lonely figure in the gold balconied box. Then the lights began to dim and the music swelled up, delicate threads of sound becoming full-blooded melody that drew all those present into a shared experience.

Kate knew, seconds after the curtain rose, that she would never be able to describe the performance adequately for Miss Redvers. The tiny figure in the long tutu of white net, swans' feathers ringing her crown of black hair, was not living flesh and blood but some ideal of perfect beauty that was briefly glimpsed and then withdrew, fragile as gossamer. As Odette Kschessinska was the dream every man holds in his heart with all the sadness of mortality in drooping limbs and head. As Odile, glittering in black jet, she was that same beauty twisted into something cold and evil like dark ice under a moonless sky. Kate forgot herself and her surroundings and was caught up in the drama and poetry as the music and the dancer soared and swooped, becoming part of the same indefinable essence.

'Will you adjourn to the bar?'

Serge's voice seemed to come from a great distance and she blinked aware with a little shock that the house lights were going up and people were beginning to rise.

'I'll stay here,' she said, dragging her attention back with difficulty. 'I don't want to—to lose any of it.'

To her relief he seemed to understand her meaning without any further explanation.

'I'll get some champagne,' he said, rising and going to the back of the box.

When it came she sipped it in a daze, her eyes still clouded with the images of bird maidens and handsome archers.

'Kschessinska is in excellent form,' Serge said. 'In three or four years she may be more technically perfect but tonight she is the embodiment of youthful grace.'

'I shall never forget this,' Kate breathed. 'When I am an old lady I'll tell my grandchildren, if I have any, that I saw Kschessinska dance Swan Lake at the Maryinski Theatre in St Petersburg!'

'Cousin, will you take some advice?' Serge asked abruptly.

'What?' She glanced at him over the rim of her glass.

'Go home to England,' he said. 'No, let me finish! I didn't want you to come in the first place. The Narodnys are an ancient and a proud family and your very existence strains the record. It may be foolish and cruel but it is the way things are in old Russia. My brother is more French in his tastes and too inexperienced to understand. An illegitimate girl can never be anything but an embarrassment in the social world. She has no rights in law and little chance of finding a husband. To be honest I expected a cheap little fortune-hunter but I was wrong. Whatever happened between your mother and my uncle, it's clear that you're a spirited young lady, and a sensitive one. If you stay in Russia you will be badly hurt. I don't want that to happen to you.'

'It need not,' she argued. 'Aunt Natalya invited me and is ready to welcome me as a member of the family.'

'It would be wiser for you to go home,' he repeated. 'Believe me, cousin, but there is nothing for you here.'

'Perhaps what I want isn't what you'd expect,' she said, keeping her temper with difficulty. 'I am not here to claim my rights in law, or to catch a husband as you elegantly phrase it. I wanted to find my roots—my father's roots if you like! My job has been kept open for me at the school, so you needn't fear I'll stay long.'

'If you stay much longer,' he said, 'I will try to make you my mistress.'

'Is that intended as a threat or a promise?' she flashed.

'A statement of fact,' he said. 'You're not beautiful, but there is a cool, enigmatic quality about you that contrasts with your spurts of hot temper in a most piquant way. You interest me, cousin.'

'The interest certainly isn't mutual,' she said icily, 'so you may abandon that idea at once. And I've no intention of going home yet. It would be the height of bad manners to return to England without meeting Aunt Natalya when she invited me to come to Russia in the first place, so you may save your breath and keep your insults to yourself.'

'It was a friendly warning,' he said.

Kate turned her shoulders towards him, opening her fan and using it energetically. It was dreadful, but beneath her anger at his insulting suggestion ran a vein of excitement.

The lights were dimming again and she fixed her eyes on the rising curtain, striving to lose herself again in the magic of the ballet. It was a tribute to the excellence of the performance that she was again snared by the beauty unfolding before her.

The evening ended to thunderous applause as the tiny ballerina took her curtain calls. Alone on the stage, flowers showering about her, she raised her white arms and curtsied deeply to the royal box where her lover sat, applauding with the rest.

To her surprise Kate discovered that her cheeks were wet. The ballet had moved her profoundly but more meaning was given to the tale of the bird maiden and the prince by the fact that in real life there would be no happy ending. Kschessinska would be pensioned off and her lover would marry a German princess.

'If you wish we can go on to the Restaurant Cuba for supper,' Serge said.

'Thank you, but I promised Uncle Alexis that I'd go straight home,' she said.

'Oh, I feared that you might turn into a swan or something at midnight.'

'If that's true then you had better take heed. Swans can peck,' she said, accepting her cloak with as much cool dignity as she could muster.

'You're a very obstinate young woman,' he said, frowning slightly.

'Because I won't slink back to England with my tail between my legs?' She faced him with her head high and the glints flashing in her eyes like yellow sparks. 'You had better understand, *cousin,* that your threats and insults won't make the slightest difference. I am staying in Russia until I decide to leave and when I do it won't be because of you.'

'Then we'll call a truce,' he said, putting out his hand. 'I won't try to drive you away and you will admit that you sometimes act impulsively without due thought for the consequences.'

'Very well.'

It was foolish to keep up the quarrel and sour the evening. Reluctantly she allowed his hand to clasp her own. His fingers were long, the skin slightly roughened. It was the hand of an active man, she thought, and wondered what it would feel like to have those hands stroke her bare flesh.

'Mind, I shall still try to seduce you,' he said softly.

'You'd be wasting your time,' she said coolly, withdrawing her hand.

'You might find Narodnia boring,' he countered, opening the door for her with an exaggerated politeness.

In the carriage she sat aloofly, her eyes turned towards the snowflakes drifting down and swirling in little gusts of wind under the horses' hooves. There was a long line of coaches and red-painted sleighs outside the theatre and a chorus of good night greetings rang through the air.

Serge took his place beside her, tucking a fur rug around them both. She stole a glance at his hawk-like profile and felt again that queer prickling of excitement along her nerves.

'We will drive home along the banks of the river,' he said. 'In the event of your having grandchildren there is one sight that you must boast of having seen.'

They were driving slowly away from the twinkling lights that outlined the façades of the varicoloured buildings. Serge leaned up to rap sharply on the roof and the carriage rolled to a stop.

'Look out there,' he invited, stretching across her to roll down the window.

Gasping a little as she breathed in the cold blast of air, Kate did as she was bidden. The great length of shining ice below the stone parapet was a medley of brilliant colours. Pink, blue and gold played like living patterns over the shining surface and above the night sky was a blaze of pastel.

'It's—' She stopped, partly because she was at a loss for words, partly because he was kissing her, turning her away from the colour into the darkness of his embrace.

'Now you can tell your grandchildren,' he said, signalling the driver to move on as he released her, 'that you were kissed very thoroughly by the light of the aurora borealis.'

Shivering, she jerked away from him and sat bolt upright in her corner of the carriage, turning her face to the icy breeze that blew through the still open window. If she yielded in any way then he would have every excuse for holding a low opinion of her but her shivering was perilously close to desire.

FIVE

Although she would not have admitted it Kate felt a small stab of disappointment when they set out the next morning. Serge had bidden her a formal good-night in the courtyard and crunched off into the snow, presumably to his own lodgings. There was no sign of him as she took her place in the hooded troika and she was too proud to enquire if he would be accompanying them.

Marisa sat beside her with Anton driving and a second sleigh was piled with luggage, among which she glimpsed her own leather portmanteau. The Count and Peter were riding horseback and the bustle of departure evidently engaged their full attention for the Count grunted a greeting and Peter merely lifted his hand.

Despite her thick travelling coat and heavy scarf she was glad of the fleecy rugs tucked almost to her chin. Marisa had handed her a jar of cream and a peaked visor of shaded glass, with the information that she had best grease her face and tie on the eyeshade.

'Otherwise your skin will be raw and your eyes inflamed. It takes time for a foreigner to become accustomed to our climate,' she finished.

'Thank you. That's very kind.' Kate hoped Marisa was beginning to unbend a little but the older woman said frostily:

'Mademoiselle Natalya instructed me to see to your comfort on the journey.'

Her expression proclaimed clearly that,

left to herself, she would cheerfully have flung Kate out of the sleigh and abandoned her to die of frostbite.

Kate obediently covered her face with the cream and pulled on the eyeshade. The air, as Marisa had warned, was sharp and stinging and gusts of snow blew through the open sides of the hood. It was still quite dark though Kate glanced at her watch saw that it was just nine. Days were short here, for she had noticed twilight stealing in around three o'clock.

'We reach the monastery in five or six hours unless a blizzard comes,' Marisa said, evidently reading her mind.

'Is it possible to get lost?' Kate ventured.

'The trail is marked,' Marisa said briefly. 'The Narodny family has been travelling between St Petersburg and Narodnia for five generations.'

Kate wanted to ask more questions but the housekeeper, having volunteered the information, closed her eyes and leaned her head back against the padded cushions with the evident intention of not indulging in any more conversation.

They had left the city and were speeding over a featureless white plain across which the wind blew strongly under a slowly lightening sky. Once she had become accustomed to the swift, gliding motion Kate began to enjoy herself. There was space all about her, the whiteness of the horizon merging into the pearl grey of the sky. Nothing marred the untrodden waste but at intervals a large black stone was set deep in the ice, obviously to mark the trail. Overhead a flock of wild geese flew with outstretched necks, uttering their weird, honking cry.

Imperceptibly the landscape was altering, the level ground becoming gentle slopes, the whiteness varied by dark green and an occasional flash of red as pine and holly thrust up bravely through the snow.

Her uncle and cousin had been riding ahead but Peter turned and trotted back towards the sleigh, leaning from the saddle to say loudly:

'Two hours more and we'll be at the monastery. We're making excellent time.'

They slowed down as they entered the forest proper, the trail narrowing and twisting between the trees, the horses forced to a walking pace as they negotiated the steep gullies. It was as dim in the forest as if it were still night and she took off the hampering visor and bathed her eyes in the cool green light filtering down through the leaves.

Sunlight, bright and blinding, seared her gaze as they emerged from the shelter of the trees and she shielded her face with her hands against the icy wind as they dipped down into the valley. Below them was a huddled mass of stone surmounted by a high tower on which a golden weathercock turned. As they came closer she saw wooden buildings built up against the surrounding walls, seeming to lean against them for protection. Fur-clad figures padded towards them across the snow and there was smoke issuing from the chimneys of the various dwelling-places. They drove through open gates into a courtyard where a tall man in a black habit under a furred cloak came to greet them, his long thin hand raised palm outwards as he said in a voice that sounded harsh as if from disuse:

'*Kak dyela! Stras vitye?*'

Marisa answered him in Russian and was obviously explaining Kate's presence for he gave several curious glances in her direction. The Count had already gone within the main building but Peter had dismounted and now came to her side.

'Come inside, cousin. This part of the monastery is for the general public and is run by the lay brothers. The enclosure where the monks live is in another wing and forbidden to the secular.'

She allowed him to help her down and leaned against him briefly, stamping her feet to restore the circulation.

The stone building looked forbidding with its steep gables and narrow windows but, within, a long, low room was warm and lamplit, with fires blazing at both ends of it and a huge table already laid.

Her uncle was warming his hands at one of the fires but turned as they came in, saying in a tone that suggested his humour had improved:

'We've made excellent time. It is not yet dark. Come to the fire, Kate. They are preparing a room for you and the meal will be on the table in a moment.'

'Is this the refectory?' Kate asked.

'Only for the guests. The monks eat in their own quarters. I'm afraid the conditions are fairly primitive but this is a simple hostelry for travellers. Most of them are bound for Archangel. Ah! the food is ready. Shall we take our places?'

He was escorting her to the table with

a geniality that seemed unforced.

'You're happy to be going back to Narodnia,' she said with sudden insight.

'Indeed I am. Peter here would take issue with me on that subject.'

'Not this time,' the younger man said. 'I'm quite ready to go for the rest of the season for the pleasure of my new cousin's company.'

'Kate may not care to stay long in the depths of the country,' her uncle said.

'Then I'll whisk her back to St Petersburg and we'll dance away the summer,' Peter said.

'It would serve the family better if you paid more heed to the estate,' the Count said, his voice sharpening.

'I leave that to Serge,' Peter said, unabashed. 'What do you think of the soup, Kate?'

It had been served by two lay brothers and was steaming hot, its flavour peppery. There were two dishes heaped with fish in the centre of the table and a bowl of shiny red apples, with side dishes of pickled vegetables.

'It's warming,' she said cautiously.

'Russian meals are generally heavily

flavoured,' Peter said. 'I prefer French cuisine myself.'

'Your mother did too.' His father's voice had softened slightly. 'She always loved everything French.'

'Then I take after her,' Peter said.

'At Narodnia we eat Russian food.' The Count cleared his throat as if he were closing a door into the past. 'My mother and I prefer the old ways.'

'Medieval,' Peter said under his breath with a laughing glance at Kate.

The tall thin monk had entered and now leaned over the Count's chair and spoke to him in a low voice.

'Brother Nicholas wishes to know if you would like to see your room,' her uncle said.

'Yes, please.' Kate rose at once, hoping there would be hot water. Despite the cream her face felt tight and stretched.

The monk led her in silence up a flight of steps and through a maze of narrow corridors into a tiny room that couldn't have been larger than one of the enclosure cells. Here he left her, still without a word. Kate wondered if the vows he'd taken precluded his talking to a female and then remembered that he had spoken to Marisa, so it was probable he couldn't speak English.

The room was simple stone with woven matting on the floor and a lantern hanging from the ceiling. The bed was built into a kind of cupboard in the wall and there were furs piled upon it. A jug of hot water and a folded towel were on a broad sill next to a deep basin and in the corner was a three-legged stool.

Kate took off her hat and scarf but decided not to risk taking off her coat for the room was unheated. She washed her face and rebraided her hair, coiling it over her ears in a simple style her mother had favoured, which she also trusted would keep her ears warmer.

Somewhere in the depths of the monastery a bell was ringing. She went out into the passages again and tried to retrace her steps back to the main guest hall but the corridors twisted and turned, branching off to left and right and doubling back on themselves in the most confusing manner. The only light came from flaring sconces set high in the walls and an icy blast whistled through the narrow slit windows.

Kate had begun to think that she was doomed to wander for ever in the labyrinth of stone when a faint but unmistakable sound of chanting came to her ears. She had reached the top of a narrow flight of steps that spiralled down into darkness and she went down cautiously, feeling for footholds on the worn stone. Her hands touched a wooden surface and she felt a latch under her fingers. The latch lifted easily and she stepped into a dazzle of light and colour blended with spiralling clouds of incense and the rhythmic chanting of an unseen choir.

This was obviously the church and a service was in progress. Kate walked as softly as her boots would permit down the side aisle and slipped into one of the high, carved pews. Ahead of her the high altar glittered in the light of hundreds of candles that struck fire from the gems that edged the great crucifix suspended apparently in space over the jewelled rood screen. Against the dark, polished stone of the columns that soared up to the vaulted roof stood bearded monks, swinging gold censors in a woven pattern of fragrance.

Kate sat, fascinated by the spectacle which was so theatrical that it bore no relation to any church service she had ever attended. The congregation was as fascinating as the priests and monks who passed and repassed one another in what reminded her of the page of some living Book of Hours. There were several of the lay brothers kneeling with bent heads, a number of men in patched and shabby clothes and a sprinkling of peasant women wrapped in heavy shawls with wooden rosaries dripping through their fingers. There was an ancient and terrible patience in their seamed faces and their clear eyes were raised to the rich glory of the altar. It was evident that the strange and elaborate ritual meant something very special to them.

The service was drawing to its close and the congregation was rising to its feet, shuffling forward to the altar. Kate had intended to remain where she was but a dark shawled woman was poking her in the ribs and muttering something incomprehensible and she obediently fell in with the rest, moving forward into the radiance of the candles. She could see from those in front that as each person reached the altar steps he knelt, tilting back his head while a priest in a stiffly embroidered cope of gold and silver brocade traced a cross on the worshipper's forehead.

Her turn came and she knelt, raising her face. The priest, thumb crooked, paused, staring down at her, and she saw shock and consternation chase across his bearded face. Then he bent, tracing the cross firmly on her brow. She was aware of the pressure of his thumb and heard, below the high chanting, his voice, low, urgent, speaking English.

'Go back, Mademoiselle Rye. Go back.'

Kate opened her mouth to demand his meaning but he had stepped aside and another priest was beckoning forward the woman behind her.

She rose and went thoughtfully to the side altar where a halo of candles surrounded a silver ikon of the Madonna who stood, in rigid Byzantine style, flanked by enamelled lilies.

'Beautiful, isn't it?' a voice said in her ear.

Kate jumped violently and swung around to face Serge whose brilliant eyes smiled down at her in familiar mockery.

'You here,' she said blankly.

'I rode ahead of you,' he said, putting his arm around her and turning her to face the altar again. 'What do you think of the Madonna?'

'Exquisite and remote,' she said slowly.

'She was the Narodnys' gift to the monastery more than a hundred years ago,' he said. 'Well, not exactly a gift. Gregoire Narodny was given shelter here when he was a poor young man on his way to make his fortune in the city. He made his fortune and had the ikon made and given to the monks on permanent loan. There is a copy of it in our own chapel at Narodnia.'

'It is beautiful,' she said slowly.

'Legends have grown up about it,' he said, lowering his voice and ushering her to the side as the various members of the congregation began to tramp out. 'It's said that if a maiden lights three candles here on the night of the rising moon she will bear a child within the year.'

'Oh!' Kate gave the ikon a nervous look and backed away slightly.

'There's a rising moon tonight,' her cousin said softly.

'Then I must take care not to light any candles,' she retorted.

'I am beginning to think it will be amusing to have you at Narodnia for a while,' he said.

'The priest here told me to go back,'

she said impulsively.

'What on earth do you mean?' She had startled him in her turn.

'He told me to go back. When I went up for the blessing he told me to go back.'

'You must have been mistaken,' he said.

'He spoke English,' she insisted, 'and he used my name. Did you mention it to anyone? You arrived before we did.'

'I've not mentioned your name to anyone,' he frowned. 'My horse was favouring her leg a little and I've been out in the stables with her.'

'He called me by my name and told me to go back,' she repeated and shivered violently as if someone had laid a cold finger along her spine.

'I can make enquiries if it troubles you,' he began.

'It doesn't matter. Perhaps I did imagine it,' she said slowly.

'It doesn't sound like something you could have imagined,' Serge said.

'Perhaps he knew my mother,' she said.

'Are you like her?'

'Not identical but there's a resemblance and she wore her hair in this fashion. She probably stayed here on her way to Narodnia.'

'And the reverend father had the shock of his life when you trotted up the aisle for his blessing. He probably thought you were a ghost.'

But the priest had looked at her as if he knew exactly who she was and his muttered words had been a warning.

'Come back to the fire,' Serge said, 'unless you are minded to light a candle!'

'No, thank you,' she said hastily.

'Come and have a glass of tea then, with a sip of vodka in it to put the colour back into your face.'

'Don't mention my foolishness to Uncle Alexis,' she said as they paced to the double doors.

'I owe you a favour for not telling father about my boorish conduct at the railway station,' he said, pressing her arm slightly.

Kate was not sure if she relished a conspiracy with the cousin whose intentions towards her were far from clear but she went with him unresisting down another tangle of corridors and into the main hall again.

'Serge! Nobody told us you were here!' Peter exclaimed, jumping up from the bench where he was sitting.

'I rode on ahead, but I'll accompany you the rest of the way. Good-evening, Father. You missed a splendid performance last night. Kschessinska was marvellous.'

They lapsed into Russian while Kate accepted a glass of steaming tea from Peter and sat near the crackling fire.

'Where did you vanish?' Peter enquired, sitting next to her.

'I found the church and stayed for the service. It was beautiful,' she said. 'Strange and beautiful.'

'Orthodox,' he nodded. 'You'll be Church of England?'

'In a tepid way.'

'I like the Lutheran services myself,' he said in a low voice, glancing towards the others. 'Father would have a heart attack if he heard me say that. We Narodnys have always been devout churchmen.'

'Serge was telling me about the ikon—the Madonna on permanent loan to the monastery.'

'Ah, my ancestor was a cautious man. Not an outright gift, you see, but a loan, designed to make the good brothers grateful for generations to come. The monastery fulfils a service though it has become quite famous for its hospitality.'

'I shall be glad to get to Narodnia,' she said. 'Suddenly, despite everything, I feel as if I'm going home. Is that foolish?'

'I'm glad you feel like that,' he said promptly. 'I think you should be acknowledged fully as a member of the family. My father and Serge are too hidebound in their ways.'

"But they have begun to accept me," Kate thought. "They have both begun to realise that I am not the little fortune-hunter they expected."

'We leave at first light, so you would do well to get a good night's sleep,' her uncle said, coming across to her.

'If I can find my room again,' she said, putting down her empty glass and rising.

'Marisa will know it. She has the room next to yours,' he said.

The housekeeper, who had been sitting by the fire at the other end of the room, rose at his beckoning hand and took a candle from the table.

'You would be wise to sleep in your clothes, Mademoiselle,' she said as they traversed the corridors together. 'It is a bitter night and the bedchambers are unheated.'

'Marisa, my mother would have stayed

here on her way to Narodnia, I suppose?'
Kate said abruptly.

'It's the only stopping-place,' Marisa
said.

'And when she left Narodnia?'

'She would have stayed here then, too.'

Kate frowned, knowing there was a
question to be asked but not certain what
it was.

'Good-night, Mademoiselle.' Marisa set
down the candle and went out.

Kate took off her coat and boots and
wrapped one of the furs about herself
and snuggled down in the narrow bed.
There were two hot, smooth stones at the
bottom and she curled her toes around
them, pulled the heavy blankets up to
her neck and fell asleep to the guttering
of the candle. Once or twice in her sleep
she was conscious of a bell ringing, half
woke to wonder if the monks were being
summoned to prayer and slept again.

Marisa roused her, bringing hot water
and a mug of the steaming tea that
every inhabitant of the country seemed
to drink in vast quantities. When she was
fully dressed again she went, cautiously
following her nose, down to the main hall.
The fires had been lit and a substantial

meal had been laid on the table. The three men were already booted and spurred and greeted her briefly as she took her place.

'Blinis,' Peter said, passing her some of the hot wafer-thin pancakes.

Kate found that she was hungry and applied herself with enthusiasm to the filling breakfast. Through the half-open door she could see a fragile sun turning the snow in the courtyard into gold. The sky above was a pale, newly washed blue.

'Is your horse better?' she remembered to ask Serge.

'Fine. It's my opinion she was faking in the hope of a good rest,' he said.

'All females are natural actresses,' the Count said.

He was baiting her, Kate knew, but there was no real malice in his voice.

He seemed to have mellowed as they travelled further away from St Petersburg. Kate wondered if the glittering, fairy-tale city reminded him too keenly of his dead wife.

The troikas were waiting, the horses already harnessed. Kate had spread some of the protective cream over her face and she pulled down the eyeshade to shield her eyes from the glare of sun on snow. One or two of the lay brothers were in the yard, carrying in bundles of wood, but there was no sign of the priest she had seen the previous night.

At the open gate some children were tumbling about in the snow, their laughter shrill, their breath weaving white spirals in the clear air. The Count checked his mount and threw a handful of coins among them and his sons followed suit. The children scrambled for the money, rolling over and over in the snow, while several women, their feet tied up in sacking and strips of fur, ran from the wooden huts to scoop up as many of the coins as they could.

'*Moujika!*' Marisa said, compressing her mouth. 'Dirty peasants!'

'They look very poor,' said Kate.

'As God wills,' the housekeeper said. 'We cannot all be rich, Mademoiselle, and these are lucky. They live close by the monastery and rely on the monks for help.'

They bowled through gates into a white world that stretched endlessly in every direction. Even the black trail-markers had become pillars of ice. Snuggled in her furs Kate forgot the poverty she had seen in the wonder of so much sparkling brilliance.

Abruptly the horizon darkened into forest again. Tall conifers reared their proud heads into the sky and cast long shadows over the white ground. Serge rode back towards the sleigh, bending to speak to her. He had no need of protective cream or visors, Kate thought, glancing up at his wind-tanned features and narrow, brilliant eyes. This setting was his true element and he fitted it as easily as any wild creature adapts itself to an untamed landscape.

'Are you frozen?' he enquired.

'Warm as toast. When do we reach the estate?'

'You have been riding across it for the last couple of hours,' he said.

'Oh!' She uttered the word with awe and he laughed, his hard face creasing into mirth.

'Three thousand acres,' he said. 'We used to own four hundred serfs too. That was before my time. The serfs were freed nearly thirty years ago by the Tzar Alexander the Second but they continue to serve the Narodnys. Another hour and you will see the roof of the house below as you reach the crest of the rise.'

The horses were floundering in the deep snow and he broke off, riding to the lead horse and tugging at its rein while Anton leapt from the driving seat and went round to the other side to help.

The forest was thinning out, the steep path becoming a gently sloping plateau. Away to the right sunlight gleamed on an expanse of ice. She wondered briefly if that was the lake on which her father had skated to his death and then, turning her head, she saw before her, shining in the sun, the high roofs of an immense and sprawling building and knew they had come to Narodnia.

SIX

The house was a series of buildings, linked by courtyards and covered passages. There was no wall around the whole but a line of firs screened it from the east wind. The high roof had tall chimneys and slanted down to one side almost to the ground. At the front narrow windows reflected the afternoon light and cast lozenges of colour across the snow.

'The roof is mainly copper,' Serge said. He had slowed to a walking pace and rode beside the sleigh. 'It withstands the worst weather.'

'It's—fantastic,' Kate said. She had been going to say 'beautiful' but that wasn't the right word for the baroque grandeur spread out before them.

'We'll be there soon.' He touched spurs to his mount and rode ahead.

The doors of the main façade of the building were faced with copper too, Kate saw, and two servants in belted tunics and baggy trousers were hurrying out as the sleigh drew to a halt. She was helped out and bustled into a wide corridor flooded by sunshine with a row of arched doors opposite. The central one was open, revealing a hall with twin staircases winding to a gallery above. Kate had a confused impression of an enormous fireplace in which flames roared and glowed, of lamps hung against dark wood, of a servant offering her a small glass. She took it and choked on vodka, her face flushing scarlet as the burning spirit caught her throat.

'Alexis, Alexis!' The voice was high and

sweet, fluting as a bell.

'Natalya.' The Count went to the foot of one of the staircases to meet the woman coming down.

Kate, blinking back tears as the effect of the vodka wore off, saw that the woman descending was tiny, her dark hair smoothed into a chignon, her face small and pale. She wore a gown of almost unrelieved black in a cut of nunlike severity but there was a froth of silvery lace beneath her pointed chin and her eyes were a clear, light blue set above high cheekbones.

She was speaking rapidly in Russian, turning to embrace her nephews who towered over her for she was very small.

Then, hands outstretched, she came towards Kate, her face lit by a welcoming smile, her blue eyes moistening.

'And you are Katharine, my poor brother's girl! Oh, I have longed to see his child here at Narodnia. Did you have a good time in St Petersburg? I would have been there to greet you but my mother has not been well and I had to return. But you will want a hot bath and a change of clothes, my dear. I will take you up myself. The men must take care of themselves while you and I get acquainted.'

She spoke English fluently with only the faintest trace of accent and she talked very quickly, in little spurts and gasps, as if she were continually grasping at stray thoughts that eluded her. She had taken Kate's hand and was urging her towards the stairs, still chattering as they went.

'My poor brother would have been so happy to know he had a daughter. I have wondered ever since your letter came if you would resemble him but I believe that you resemble your mother more. Dear Anna! I have wondered so often what happened to her, why she left Narodnia in such haste. This is your room, my dear, with the dressing-room beyond. I hope you will be comfortable here.'

They had mounted the stairs, crossed the gallery and walked down a long corridor. The room into which they went was a high-ceilinged apartment, the mouldings picked out in gold, the walls of satiny wood against which curtains of soft apricot velvet hung, matching the curtains on the high tester bed. Rugs of brown and cream covered the polished floor and in one corner a silver samovar bubbled.

'This is one of our nicest rooms,' Aunt Natalya said. 'We have two other guest

116

suites but they face north. This one catches the first of the sun in the mornings and the last of it at night. Not that I wish you to think of yourself as a guest! You are a member of the family.'

'You're very kind,' Kate said gratefully. 'I'm afraid the news of my existence came as a disagreeable shock.'

'A surprise,' her aunt corrected. 'Oh, my brother, Alexis, is a trifle old fashioned in his ways but he is a good man. A very good man. And he cannot fail but be charmed by such a lovely young niece. And for me it is a particular pleasure to meet you. Your dear mother was my governess for more than a year, so it is almost like having her back again. Ah, Marisa! Is my niece's trunk being carried up?'

'Oui, Mademoiselle.' The housekeeper had entered and stood silently just within the door.

Kate, glancing at the two women, thought how different they were, though both wore black dresses and were roughly the same age. But the housekeeper had a cold, withdrawn expression as if any sweetness in her had long since been dried up in her while Aunt Natalya was full of gaiety and an almost girlish excitement.

117

Her smooth face was unlined, her hair raven, though she must be in her early forties.

A manservant brought in the portmanteau and was followed by two maidservants carrying pails of hot water.

'I will leave you to bath and change,' Aunt Natalya said. 'Anna will come and show you the way to the dining-room. Oh, but we shall have so much to talk about.'

She pressed Kate's hands and went out, followed by Marisa.

Kate noticed that the light outside the windows was beginning to fade into a swift twilight but the lamps were lit in her room and in the adjoining dressing-room where the two little maids were pouring the water into a hipbath. They ducked out, giggling behind their hands, closing the door softly behind them.

She took off her garments and stepped into the hot water, relaxing into it thankfully. The long hours in the troika had been more cramping than she realised and she flexed her muscles under the water, letting the stiffness drain out of her.

The evening dress would hardly do for another night in a row and it was not likely that the family would wear full dress at a private dinner. Or so Kate hoped, as she took a simple gown of creamy wool from the portmanteau. With its wide, dipping collar and long floating sleeves and skirt it was deceptively modest but when she moved her long limbs were outlined under the clinging fabric.

She was coiling up her hair when there was a tap on the door and a plump girl with reddish hair curling over her shoulders came in. She was not pretty but there was the charm of youth in her face and her ruffled blue dress was of the latest fashion.

'You must be Anna?' Kate put out her hand cordially.

'I am Anna Nicholaevna Verotsky,' the girl said, dropping a curtsey without seeming to notice the proffered hand. 'Mademoiselle Natalya told me to show you the way to the dining-room.'

She spoke without expression, her eyes downcast. Kate wondered if she were extremely shy or if she disliked her for some reason.

'You are my uncle's ward, I believe,' she said.

'Yes. The Count is my guardian,' the

girl said briefly. 'This way, Mademoiselle.'

Feeling rebuffed, Kate followed her along the passage and down the second of the twin staircases.

'This way.' Anna spoke without turning her head as she rustled down another corridor into a high-ceilinged room hung with crimson. Dozens of tiny copper lamps cast a rosy glow over the embroidered rugs that were flung in apparent casual disorder over the floor.

The Count and his two sons had changed into the high-necked, belted tunics and long trousers that seemed to be standard Russian dress and it suited the elder two. Peter, however, looked faintly ill at ease as if he had put on a fancy dress.

'So you and Anna found each other!' Aunt Natalya exclaimed, coming forward with her little rushing step. 'This is such an immense place that it's easy to get lost but the family quarters are really quite compact. The servants' wing takes up a great deal of space and Marisa has a flat to herself over the kitchens and then my mother has her own suite.'

'I would like to meet her,' Kate broke in.

'She retires very early but tomorrow we

shall make the grand tour. Shall we take our seats? You must all be starving!'

A long table at one end of the room was laid with white cloths and heavily embossed silver cutlery. There was none of the lightness and gaiety of the St Petersburg house here but there was an enduring richness. Taking her place next to Peter, Kate had a feeling of permanence, of an endless succession of families sitting down to dine in this red and silver room.

Serge was opposite her, next to Anna, and she sensed his eyes on her, watching and evaluating her reactions. Next to him the girl sat silent, toying nervously with a fork. For two people intended to marry they showed little interest in each other.

Marisa didn't appear. Instead a succession of dishes was carried in by an unending stream of servants. Kate, working her way conscientiously through a varied and spicy menu, ventured to enquire:

'Have you a large staff, then?'

'Twenty or thirty indoors. They keep the place running. The outside workers live about a mile off, at the other side of the lake,' the Count said.

'Is it a farm then?' she asked.

'We grow a few crops for our own

needs but the main wealth of the estate lies in timber.' It was Serge who answered, his hard face kindling with enthusiasm. 'We have fine trees here and room to plant more. Much of it is cut down indiscriminately and wasted. A good deal is taken up to Archangel and shipped abroad. We have a sawmill on the eastern range.'

'Serge has ideas for expanding,' the Count said.

'Not expanding but contracting,' Serge said. 'At the moment we supply wood—raw materials for others to fashion. We could cut down the trees and provide work for our own people by designing furniture. There are craftsmen at Narodnia who are artists in their own right. They make chairs, stools, tables for their own homes that would stand comparison with the best anywhere in the world. We could extend their activities, set up a cottage industry, train others. We could make Narodnia—'

'A kind of factory,' Peter said. 'Well, you may do as you please, my dear brother, provided you let me have the house in St Petersburg and half the profits!'

'You can earn your share of the profits,' Serge retorted. 'I'll need a sales representative to travel to all the capitals of the world and convince them that Narodnia furniture if the best in the whole of Russia.'

'And while you carve up the estate between you, kindly remember that I am not yet dead,' the Count rumbled.

'We could begin now,' Serge began but his aunt's voice cut in.

'I positively forbid any more discussion of this dreadful subject tonight! You must be boring Katharine to death!'

'I think it's fascinating,' Kate began but Aunt Natalya shook her black head in laughing reproof.

'If you allow them they will argue for ever! The young always want to change things, haven't you noticed? I suppose that I was the same once.'

'My dear Natalya, you speak as if you were in your dotage,' her brother chided.

'Perhaps it is because I was so happy during my girlhood.' She gave a fluttering little sigh and rushed on. 'Do you remember how it was when father was alive? The balls and the suppers and the big sleighing parties? I was allowed to stay up late for those and then you and I and Boris used to creep up to bed with our pockets full of sweetmeats and listen to the music still drifting up from below! Oh, they were such happy days, Katharine. My mother was so gay and my father such a distinguished man.'

'From what I recall of grandfather,' Serge put in, 'he was the most dreadful bully. Six feet tall and broad as a bull with a roar to match and a hairtrigger temper. I was thirteen when he died, Kate, and I tell you that a heartfelt sigh of relief ran round the community.'

'Alexis, speak to him,' Aunt Natalya begged. 'He mustn't be allowed to say such things about Father! The master of the house must be true master else he will forfeit respect.'

'Truth is more important,' Serge said, a flush on his high cheekbones. 'When a man dies he doesn't automatically become a saint.'

'My father had his good points,' the Count said.

'And many of them,' Aunt Natalya clucked. 'He was a fair man, a hard taskmaster but a fair one. You are too young to remember, Serge, but in his prime he was a splendid man, a most loving father.'

'And my father,' Kate said. 'What was my father like?'

There was a tiny silence and then Aunt Natalya said:

'Boris was truly a saint. Gentle and bookish—oh, he was so clever, wasn't he, Alexis?'

'Cleverer than I could ever be,' the Count agreed. 'There was only a year between us in age but he had twice as much knowledge in his head. Latin, Greek, mathematics, forever poring over his books.'

'You must get your brains from him,' Aunt Natalya said. 'You said in your letter that you taught in a school.'

'I'm not so very clever,' she said.

'Nonsense, my dear! I'm sure you're very clever,' Aunt Natalya leaned and patted her hand consolingly.

'She's certainly an independent young woman,' Uncle Alexis said. 'You'd never have had the courage to travel so far from home all by yourself, eh, Natalya?'

'I have never wished to leave Russia,' she answered, 'but if the opportunity had arisen I trust that I would have had the necessary courage.'

'Here's to the unexplored heroism of

Natalya Petrova Narodny,' Serge said, raising his glass in an ironic little gesture.

'Serge loves to tease,' Aunt Natalya said, laughingly. 'You will have to cure him of that, Anna!'

The girl said nothing but hung her head a little lower as if she longed for the gift of invisibility.

Kate, in an effort to divert attention, said, 'I fear I would never have ventured so far without your kind invitation, Aunt Natalya.'

'Oh, but Boris was my brother and your place is here,' the other said.

'For a visit. My job is being held open for me.'

'We shall see. Narodnia lays its spell on those who come here,' Aunt Natalya said.

'Not on me, Aunt. I prefer the city any day,' Peter said.

'So do I,' Anna said.

'Silly child! You've never been to St Petersburg,' Aunt Natalya said. 'When you are married then you can be presented at Court and we will all be so proud to see you make your curtsey to the Tzar.'

'Unmarried girls go to Court, don't they?' Kate asked in surprise.

'Some do and waste the best years of

their lives in ridiculous flirtations with young officers who could never afford to marry them. It is so much wiser for a girl to learn how to be a good wife before she is launched into society,' Aunt Natalya said.

'You never married.' Kate had not intended to speak so abruptly but the gaze her aunt turned on her was gentle.

'I was only sixteen when Boris died and then a week later poor Olga too. My mother was heartbroken, quite unable to manage. The boys were left motherless so young—Serge only three years old and Peter a few months. Father told me then that the family would never have got through that dreadful year if it hadn't been for my help.'

'And helping became a habit. We have all taken advantage of that ever since,' the Count said, smiling at her.

'And when have I ever complained?' she retorted. 'Why, I cannot imagine living anywhere but at Narodnia or giving my affection to a single man when I have an entire family! My annual trips to St Petersburg perk me up for the rest of the year but I still love Narodnia best. In that Serge and I are in accord, even though he hangs fire over the wedding.'

'There is not even a betrothal yet,' Serge said, his face settling into lines of displeasure.

'You must make haste,' his aunt teased, 'or Anna will be snatched up by some other young man!'

'Anna is scarce seventeen. Give her time to make up her own mind,' Peter said.

'Young girls ought to be guided by their elders,' his father said. 'As Anna's guardian I am obliged to consult her future.'

'And the Verotskys were such a wealthy family,' Serge said, his tone suddenly savagely gibing. 'It would never do to let all those roubles slip out of the family.'

Kate gave him an icy look of contempt. She would have slapped his face if he had made such a remark in reference to her but Anna seemed not to mind.

'Coffee, in the drawing-room,' Aunt Natalya said. 'Alexis, you'll not sit too long over your brandy.'

She rose and fluttered ahead of them down another covered passage into a pleasant room, furnished in pine and hung with silky curtains in a clear pink shade like the petals of a rose. There were numerous high-backed chairs, piled with cushions in soft pastels, and tables on which china ornaments were arranged.

'This is my favourite room,' Aunt Natalya said. 'Serge declares it is too prissy and feminine but I think it's most elegant.'

'I think so too,' Kate said.

'I knew we would agree,' the older woman said happily. 'Anna, pour the coffee, my love. Come and sit next to me by the fire, Katharine—or do you prefer Kate?'

'Kate, please.' She watched Anna cross the room, the bustle of her blue dress swaying.

'She is a dear, good child,' Aunt Natalya said, lowering her voice, 'but a trifle gauche still. Her parents were very rich, you know. It will be a splendid match for Serge but he can be very obstinate. I am hoping that you being here will bring Anna out of her shell. I would like you both to be friends.'

'I'll try,' Kate said, her voice sinking a little as Anna returned with two cups of coffee. The look she gave Kate was scarcely designed to promote any kind of friendship.

'Don't you want any coffee,' Aunt Natalya enquired.

'I've had sufficient. May I be excused now?' Anna asked, standing rigidly before them.

'Yes, of course. Good-night, my dear.' Aunt Natalya presented a smooth cheek for the girl to peck.

"And there is another one who doesn't like me," Kate thought, "Marisa, Anna, Uncle Alexis tolerates me, Peter likes me but I suspect he likes most people and Serge—" she had no idea what Serge's real opinion of her was.

Aunt Natalya had said something and she answered automatically and politely, sipping the thick, strong coffee.

A little later the three men came in and the character of the room subtly changed, becoming more masculine as if they brought with them an aura of something stronger and harsher than the rose-coloured drapes and delicate ornaments.

Kate went to put back her coffee cup and pulled back one of the long curtains that shielded the window. Reflected in the blackness of the double glass her face floated like a pale disc, framed by the coils of hair.

'Very attractive, but you could see yourself more clearly in a mirror,' Serge said, lounging up to her.

Without turning her head she said frostily, 'You were very unkind to Anna.'

'Because I am a little weary of having her pushed at me as a prospective bride,' he said.

'That's no excuse,' she said.

'I wasn't making excuses,' he said. 'Anna Nicholaevna would be far more upset if I were to begin complimenting her. She is as reluctant to marry me as I am to be tied to her. Ever since her parents were killed in a train crash when she was twelve Anna has lived here, a bait for me that I refuse to snatch at.'

'I'm really not interested,' she began.

'I was merely explaining that I'm not spoken for, so if you care to chance your luck the field is open.'

'Thank you, but I'm not entering the race.' Kate let the curtain fall with a little rattle and went over to her aunt.

'Would you excuse me if I went up to my room now?' she asked. 'I really am rather weary.'

'My dear child, we have been most neglectful!' Aunt Natalya was on her feet at once, her face full of kindly concern.

'Come along upstairs. Your bed is ready

and you can sleep until noon tomorrow if you wish. Mother is always at her brightest in the early afternoon, so you will be able to see her then.'

Chattering, she led the way back along the corridors and up the stairs to the apricot-hung room. The fire still burned brightly in the fireplace and the quilts had been turned back. The portmanteau had been unpacked, she noticed, and her travelling clothes brushed and pressed and hung in the big wardrobe.

'Shall I help you, dear?' Aunt Natalya fussed.

'I'm used to managing alone. Good-night, Aunt.'

'Good-night, my dear niece.' The older woman stood on tiptoe to brush Kate's cheek with her soft lips. 'I am so happy that you accepted my invitation. You remind me so much of your mother. But we'll talk of her tomorrow. Good-night.'

The little, black-clad figure rushed out, closing the door gently.

Kate had begun to feel genuinely tired. Her eyelids were heavy and her legs shook beneath her. The bed suddenly seemed the most tempting thing in the world and she unfastened her dress quickly and slipped thankfully between the warm sheets.

She drifted into a half-sleep, seeming at one stage to be riding in the sleigh again, bobbing gently up and down. Against her closed eyelids was the whiteness of the snow and she was struggling through it. It clung to her legs, weighing her down, hampering her every step. Over her head the setting sun blazed warmth and she held up her hand towards it and breathed in—the scent of woodsmoke.

Icy water cascaded over her head and neck and she woke, coughing and choking, struggling as she was dragged clear. Her eyes smarted with smoke and it was difficult to breathe. A gust of icy wind blew through the room and the curtains billowed wildly in the draught.

Strong hands shook her into consciousness and she opened her eyes painfully, blinking at Serge, who held her close to the window he had just flung wide.

'The bed? The smell?' She croaked out the words, her gaze flying to the pile of soaked and blackened hangings.

'Independent young woman or not,' Serge said, pulling her tightly against him, 'I refuse to allow you to burn yourself to a crisp on your first night in Narodnia.'

SEVEN

The others had crowded in then, exclaiming over the damage and the danger escaped. Kate had been anxiously questioned, wrapped in a blanket, given a tot of brandy, escorted to another bedroom where a fire had been lit and stone hot water bottles brought up to warm the bed.

'You set one of the candles too near the bed-curtains,' the Count said.

'And might have stifled in the smoke before you could call for help,' Aunt Natalya said, her blue eyes wide. 'It doesn't bear thinking about! Thank God Serge was in the corridor.'

'I thought I'd look in to see if Kate had everything she needed,' Serge said.

'I'm thankful you did,' Kate said and sneezed violently.

She was instantly plied with more brandy, Aunt Natalya shooing out the men and bringing a dry nightgown. There was no sign of Anna. Presumably the girl slept too deeply or in too distant a room to have heard the commotion.

Kate took longer to fall asleep again when the others had finally departed. If Serge had not come in she might very well have been killed or seriously burned.

She wondered why he had decided to come. She had been too deeply asleep to hear anything at all. The long journey, the heavy meal with all the unfamiliar spices had combined to make her much sleepier than usual She pummelled the pillow irritably, trying to settle herself more comfortably, and thought suddenly of the candle placed too close to the bed-hangings. She wished she could remember clearly whether a candle had been placed too near. She would surely have noticed it and moved it to a safer distance. Miss Redvers had always impressed on them the dangers of fire. On the other hand she had been unusually exhausted and it was too ridiculous to suppose that anyone in the house could have crept in and held the flame to the edge of the curtains. Too ridiculous—Kate fell into a troubled sleep. She woke briefly as daylight stole through a gap in the curtains and burrowed deeper into the bedclothes, turning her face from the light and sleeping again more soundly than before.

She woke fully to the tinkling of teacups and the scent of hot raspberry preserve. The two little giggling maids had come in and were setting down a breakfast tray and pouring hot water into the hip-bath. Kate wondered why, with all the money apparently available, nobody had installed a proper water system to save the maids all the extra work that the fetching and carrying of buckets entailed.

The events of the previous day seemed like a vague, ill-remembered dream. When she had eaten she took a bath and, wrapping a robe about her that had been hanging on the back of the door, went in search of the other room. More by good luck than anything else she found her way through the long passages back to the room.

The burnt and sodden hangings had already been stripped and creamy silk was draped over the bed. The fireplace had been swept and the fire rekindled and the sun shone brightly through the window. There was no trace of the conflagration.

Kate picked out a simple morning dress of soft brown wool ruffled with lemon and coiled up her hair. The long sleep had refreshed her and her reflection in the mirror was bright-eyed and pink-cheeked.

There was a bell on the table and she looked at it thoughtfully, debating whether or not to ring for a servant. From the doorway a voice said primly:

'Good-morning, Mademoiselle.'

'Good-morning, Anna. Won't you please call me Kate?' she answered, repressing a start. The girl walked so quietly.

'Mademoiselle Natalya said you were almost burnt alive last night,' Anna said, coming further into the room.

'It wasn't as dramatic as that,' Kate said, disliking the avidity in the girl's plump face. 'A candle caught the edge of the hangings and Serge put it out.'

'Serge was here?'

'He put the fire out,' Kate repeated. 'Shall we go downstairs? I am anxious to meet my grandmother.'

'She's old and won't realise where you've come from,' Anna said, not moving.

'Then we shall have to explain it to her, won't we?' Kate said, sweeping past her into the corridor.

Anna followed slowly. She had obviously been instructed to show Kate over the main part of the house and was equally obviously reluctant to show her the smallest courtesy.

Kate thought she had divined the reason for it when Anna asked abruptly as they reached the lower hall.

'Mademoiselle Natalya said that you had been to the ballet with Serge.'

'To see Swan Lake,' Kate began, adding gently, 'Uncle Alexis would have taken me but he had business to attend. That was the only reason I went with Serge.'

Her soft words fell on deaf ears. Anna had swished through to an inner room where her voice was heard, speaking rapidly in Russian, with Marisa's voice answering her briefly.

'Good-morning, Marisa.' Kate spoke loudly as she entered.

'Good-morning, Mademoiselle. I trust you slept properly after last night's unfortunate occurrence,' the housekeeper said, curtseying with a stony expression.

'Very well. I believe I am to meet my grandmother this morning?'

'I will tell Mademoiselle that you are ready. Excuse me.'

Marisa went out, leaving the two girls together. Anna said, her lips pressed and her hands folded:

'Madame Ilsa Alexi Narodny is very frail and easily upset.'

'I don't intend to upset her,' Kate said briefly and went over to the window, staring out into a courtyard piled with snow. Anna evidently had warmer feelings for Serge than she betrayed. Could it have been Anna, walking so quietly, who had gone in and held the flame of the candle to the silky drapes?

'My dear Kate, I feared to wake you earlier lest you bite off my head for disturbing you,' Aunt Natalya said, hurrying in. 'Poor Boris had only one fault. He was a positive *bear* if he didn't get his full ration of sleep. Are you quite recovered from last night's dreadful experience? What a sorry welcome for you!'

'There was no harm done,' Kate said.

'But there might have been,' Aunt Natalya said. 'We'll not mention it to my mother for she is easily alarmed.'

'No, of course not,' Kate agreed.

'Come, we'll go up then. Mother likes to keep to her own wing of the house.'

Aunt Natalya put her arm around Kate and went with her through a door at the end of the apartment and along more covered passages which struck chill after

139

the warmth of the rooms.

They had reached a broad flight of steps and Anna, who had been lagging behind, suddenly picked up her skirts and ran ahead of them, calling as she went, 'Madame Ilsa Alexia! Madame!'

'She is very fond of her,' Aunt Natalya said tolerantly. 'Anna has been with us since she was twelve, you know.'

And makes it clear that she has more right than I have to be here, Kate thought, mounting the steps silently.

At the top of them a wide hallway led into a large room, hung with beautiful faded tapestries and furnished in the solid comfortable style that seemed a feature of the house.

A tall, white-haired woman with traces of beauty still in her fine-boned, wrinkled face sat in a high-backed chair by the fire. She wore a black gown in the style of thirty years before with an embroidered scarlet shawl about her shoulders. The vivid splash of colour seemed to emphasise her determination to hold on to life even as it passed her by and her dark eyes were unexpectedly piercing.

'One moment.' Aunt Natalya went to the side of the chair and bent over, whispering in Russian. Anna had seated herself on a low stool and was holding one of the old lady's hands in a tight, possessive clutch.

'I am explaining to her who you are,' Aunt Natalya said, straightening herself and beckoning Kate forward.

The old lady spoke, using the French tongue, her voice husky with age but still strong.

'So! You are the child of Boris and that governess! Why have you come?'

'To meet my father's family,' Kate said.

'Come near and let me see you. Anna, give place to my granddaughter.'

An imperious hand waved her forward as Anna slowly relinquished her seat. Kate sat down on the stool and felt her hands taken in a bony clasp.

'What is your name again?' the old woman asked.

'This is Kate, Mother. Kate Rye. I told you,' Aunt Natalya said patiently.

'Rye? That was the name of the governess,' her mother said. 'This is Boris's daughter, my own granddaughter. Her name is Katharina Borisova Narodny.'

'Not legally,' Kate said. 'My parents were not married.'

'Not married! Of course they were married! What nonsense to say that they were not married! Where is Igor? It's been a long time since Igor came. Igor Kerinsky. Why hasn't Igor been to see me?'

'You're confused, Mother,' Aunt Natalya said. 'We brought Kate to see you.'

'Kate? I don't know any Kate,' the old lady said. Her eyes had clouded and her fingers shook as they grasped Kate's hand.

'You are my grandmother, my babushka,' Kate said.

'You are like your mother,' said Madame Ilsa and for a moment her eyes were clear and kind. Then she thrust Kate's hand away and said something in Russian, her head shaking to and fro.

'We had better leave. She is not as well as we had hoped,' Aunt Natalya said. 'Perhaps she will feel more herself in a few days. This is always a sad time of year for her.'

She was guiding Kate towards the door, her face full of distress.

Kate glanced back to see that Anna had flung herself down at Madame Ilsa's feet and was whispering to her but the old lady was staring over her head at Kate

142

and the expression on her face was one of utter terror.

'I blame myself. I blame myself.' Aunt Natalya was saying as she bustled Kate down the stairs again. 'I have been trying to break the news to her for weeks. It is so difficult to know if she has grasped what is said to her.'

'Why is this a sad time of the year for her?' Kate asked.

'It is almost March,' Aunt Natalya said. 'Very near to the time when poor Boris died. She remembers still.'

'She seemed to remember my mother too.'

'Her going was also a grief,' Aunt Natalya said. 'Come and sit down for a while, my dear.'

She drew Kate into a small room, prettily furnished in soft shades of blue and warmed by the same blazing fire that she had seen in the other rooms. There was a tapestry frame in the corner and Aunt Natalya drew it towards her and worked as she talked, her little hands flashing the needle in and out of the design of birds.

'It is not a time any of us like to remember. Boris had gone out to skate on the lake. He was an expert skater. I was in the house looking after Olga. She had caught a bad chill and was a trifle feverish that day, and my mother sat up with her the whole of the previous night. It was a bright day, like today.' She glanced towards the window and sighed.

'And my mother? Where was my mother?' Kate asked.

'Somewhere in the house, I suppose. It was Marisa who came in and said she had seen Boris going towards the centre of the lake. It was growing dark by then and my mother was beginning to fret. She always did worry about Boris more than she worried about any of us. When darkness finally came we all became anxious and my father sent out a party with flares to search. They found his hat. Near to the hole in the ice where he had gone down. It was so dreadful that he should have died in such a way! And there was no hope of recovering his body until spring. We tried to keep the news from Olga but she gleaned it from one of the servants and I fear that the shock, in her weakened condition—' Her voice trailed away and her blue eyes were wet with tears.

'My mother—she must have been very upset!' Kate exclaimed.

'She was one of the household,' Aunt Natalya said, frowning slightly. 'Oh, I was very fond of her. She was almost like one of the family. But when it all happened we were selfishly occupied with our own grief. If I had even guessed that she and poor Boris—but we none of us knew. Olga died and Alexis was in a terrible state and Mademoiselle Anne left. She didn't even give notice to Father.'

'How did she leave?' Kate asked.

'On horseback. She paid one of the villagers to escort her. It was three days before we heard what had happened. Olga's funeral was being prepared and there were the two boys to look after and poor Boris still under the ice. My father was furious when he learned that she'd gone and I was so unhappy. I was only sixteen and she had been more friend than governess.'

Yet she had left in haste, riding back through the snow-covered wastes with only a villager to guide her. Kate's own birthday was early in October, which meant that her mother must have just begun to suspect her pregnancy when she had left Narodnia. But why leave in such desperate and secret haste? She could have worked out her month's notice and left without anyone learning of her condition. Something had frightened her, Kate decided, and she had fled but what had caused her terror remained vague and shadowy.

'Ah, well, it's a long time ago and there is no sense on dwelling on such sad events,' Aunt Natalya said briskly. 'Shall we have some lunch? The family doesn't usually gather until the evening meal, so you and I will have our meal together. Anna generally stays with my mother to keep her company.'

It was something of a relief not to have to sit down under that hostile young gaze. They had their lunch in one of the smaller apartments and Aunt Natalya chatted on brightly about her plans for the spring.

'You would not believe it now but the ground is covered with tiny wild flowers and the rivers are full of jumping fish. The days grow longer quite suddenly and at the height of summer there are only two hours of complete darkness.'

'Aunt Natalya, who was Igor Kerinsky?' Kate asked abruptly.

There was a little silence, broken only by a faint, tinkling sound as Aunt Natalya carefully laid down her fork.

'Babushka mentioned the name. Have I

146

said anything wrong?' Kate asked.

'Of course not, my dear,' the older woman smiled but there was strain in her eyes. 'Igor Kerinsky was employed here at one time. Unfortunately he stole some money. It was a great shock to my father, who had trusted him implicitly, and my mother was particularly upset.'

'Was he sent to prison?' Kate asked.

'Stealing was a capital offence,' her aunt said tightly. 'The man was hanged. It was in the summer before poor Boris died. I have thought since that that was like the overture before the curtain went up on our tragedy.'

'And my coming has reminded you all of it,' Kate said in a low voice.

'I was thrilled to learn that I had a niece,' Aunt Natalya said warmly. 'It seemed like a good omen, as if Boris had left something of himself behind as a gift to us.'

'My uncle didn't want me to come,' Kate said bluntly.

'Alexis is very old fashioned in many ways,' Aunt Natalya said. 'He believes in the honour of the family and he looked up to Boris. There was only a year between them but Boris was always clever and good, a man of very high principles. My father half hoped that he might enter the Church.'

Perhaps that was why her mother had fled, because she feared what Peter Narodny would do when he learned that his favourite son had seduced the governess.

'Alexis told me that he considers you to be a very nicely brought-up young lady,' Aunt Natalya said. 'Oh, he will come to regard you with great affection. You must be patient.'

'But I only intended this to be a visit,' Kate said. 'My job is being held open for me. I only came because I wanted to meet my father's people, to find out what he was like. I didn't even have a photograph of him.'

'None was ever taken. My father disliked the camera very much and so does my mother. He was good-looking in a gentle way. You have something of him in the way you turn your head but you are more like your mother. I wrote to her you know, after she had left, but the letter was returned, marked "Address Unknown". That hurt me a little because I thought Mademoiselle Anne was genuinely fond of me. But when your letter came it was as if my own governess had finally answered me and was coming home.'

'I'm very grateful,' Kate said.

'Nonsense,' Aunt Natalya said, leaning to pat her hand. 'It's a pleasure to have you here, and this is such a great barn of a place that we cannot possibly weary of one another's company. The men are out for much of the time and I'm occupied with my housekeeping and with caring for my mother. You saw how she was this morning.'

'May I go where I please?' Kate asked.

'Of course. Anywhere you please. This is your home while you are here, for as long as you please. I'm afraid we live quietly and don't entertain a great deal, but when the spring comes we must give some parties. Anna would like that.'

Kate doubted if Anna would like any social event if she herself were present but she smiled politely.

Lunch over, Aunt Natalya settled herself for a nap before one of the roaring fires. She couldn't be forty yet, Kate calculated, but she behaved like an elderly person. Perhaps being a spinster had something to do with it.

There was no sign of Anna or the men, which left her free to explore the house by herself. It would take more than a day, she decided within half an hour of setting off. The original mansion had been an intricate complex of rooms, staircases, passages and courtyards, added to over a couple of centuries. Staircases led up into little rooms hung with tapestries, corridors twisted back upon themselves past arched stone flagged kitchens where an army of servants seemed to be engaged in cleaning fish, preparing vegetables and chopping wood. A few of them glanced up, smiling at her shyly, and she wished she could converse with them in her father's tongue.

The short day was dawning rapidly to its close. Kate had not realised how swiftly the light dimmed nor how long the corridors were when she began to retrace her steps.

'Good-day to you, Katinka.'

Serge had stepped out of the shadows just ahead and was bowing to her with an irony that was not lost on her despite the dimness.

'My name is Kate,' she said frostily, 'and you made me jump.'

'For which I beg your pardon. I seem

to make a habit of coming upon you at unexpected moments.'

'What were you really doing in my bedroom last night?' she demanded.

'Believe it or not, but I came to make certain that you were all right.' He came closer, looking down into her face, and said, 'Are you disappointed? Did you hope I'd come to seduce you?'

'You'd have stood no chance,' she said stiffly.

'Then it's fortunate I didn't have any such intention,' he mocked. 'Have you had a good day? Did you meet Babushka?'

'She seemed confused,' Kate said.

'She often is. Don't take it to heart.' He took her hand and said, more kindly, 'Come with me and I'll show you something.'

She went with him, a little surprised to find herself so obedient, through an arched doorway and down yet another corridor to a door which he held open for her with a gallant gesture.

She passed through into an arched chapel, richly carved and lit by softly glowing lamps. There were no pews on the stone floor but there were stools and high-backed chairs set in rows down each side of a crimson carpet. The altar glittered with gold but Kate's eyes had flown to the silver Madonna who stood, flanked by lilies, in a side alcove.

'It's a copy of the one we lent to the monastery,' Serge said. 'This is only silver-plated and not as expensive.'

'She has a more friendly expression.'

Kate paused to gaze up at the calm silver features topped by a tiered crystal crown.

'She is greatly loved by the villagers,' Serge said. 'This chapel opens on to an outer yard so people may come freely in and out.'

'Are there services held here?'

'When I was a child there was a resident priest but he left to became a *starets.*'

'A what?'

'A holy man, an ascetic, who spends his life in poverty and prayer,' Serge explained. 'Such men renounce the world and wander from village to village, preaching and begging for their food. They call themselves fools of God.'

'And there are no services here now?'

Serge shook his head.

'When my uncle died my grandfather decreed the chapel would be used only for private prayer. We go to Mass to the church in the village but, as I said, people still come here to pray to the Madonna.'

'Is my father buried here?'

'The Narodnys have their own cemetery near the church. I can show it to you if you like, not today but tomorrow if the weather stays clear.'

'Yes, I'd like that.' She smiled up at him, thinking how pleasant he could be when he was in a good mood.

'And how do you like Narodnia?' he enquired.

'I haven't seen very much of it.'

'Which is a polite way of evading the question?' He lifted an arched black brow.

'Not at all, but I can't be expected to pass judgement so quickly,' Kate protested.

'And I thought you an impulsive young lady!'

'Very well. Since you ask me I think the house in St Petersburg is more elegant,' she said, 'and more convenient for the theatre and all the city amusements, but this house is more comfortable, and it has more—charm.'

'Because it isn't trying to be charming,' he said. 'It was built as a place where people were born and lived out their lives close to the land, not as a showhouse

153

where bored society folk could sit and gossip about their betters.'

'You sound passionate,' she said lightly.

'Because I feel so,' he said. 'We have taken much from the land, exploited many of its people. Now it's time to pay back. Did you know there are families in Russia who never even visit their estates? They winter in St Petersburg and go to Vienna or the South of France for their summers. They take everything and give nothing back. If I can talk Father into it I'll make all our people prosperous with the furniture we shall design and make here. No more waiting from season to season to find out if there will be feast or famine! No more indiscriminate cutting down of the pines! There will be work all the year round one day and the moujiks will hold up their heads high as fine craftsmen.'

'You make it sound as if it will really happen,' she said.

'It will.' He answered her confidently, his harsh face lively with enthusiasm. 'It must! We must pay our debt to Mother Russia or the land will turn against us and her children rise up. We have to move forward, not by trying to make ourselves mock-Europeans but by making

Russia more modern, able to take her place among the great nations of the world. Why are you smiling?'

'Because you are an astonishing person!' she exclaimed. 'You insult strange females when you are with your Cossack friends and you make political speeches in a chapel!'

'Stay with me, little Cousin,' he said, holding open the door again for her to pass through, 'and you may find yourself being continually astonished.'

EIGHT

Dinner that night was a convivial affair with both Serge and his father in an excellent humour. Only Anna, silent and downcast, failed to join in the general conversation. After the meal she and Aunt Natalya sat primly with their needlework while Peter strummed on the pianoforte and Kate was persuaded to join her voice to his. Miss Redvers had often told her that she had a tuneful voice and she sang now, aware of Serge's vivid blue eyes fixed on her in appreciation.

When she went up to her room the glowing fire and a bubbling samovar welcomed her and she fell asleep at once.

The Narodnys evidently ate breakfast in their rooms for the next morning the two giggling maidservants arrived again with a loaded tray and the buckets of hot water. Remembering that Serge had promised to take her to the village, Kate put on her travelling clothes and high boots and went downstairs in search of him. She ran him to earth in one of the drawing-rooms where, booted and cloaked, he stood talking to Aunt Natalya.

'Good-morning, my dear.' Her aunt reached up to kiss her cheek. 'Serge says you are going to ride to the village. You must wrap up warmly.'

'I'll get you an extra cloak,' Serge said. 'We'll have something to eat in the village, Aunt, so don't wait for us.'

He was ushering her out into the cold whiteness beyond the main door. She had expected to travel in the sleigh and was secretly dismayed to see a shaggy little pony saddled and waiting.

'You do ride, don't you?' Serge was wrapping a wolfskin about her shoulders.

Kate thought wryly of the sedate hours spent trotting in the local park with the senior pupils and said:

'Certainly I can!'

If she did fall off at least she would land on soft snow, she decided, allowing him to help her to the saddle.

They set off at what she was relieved to find was a steady walk. These little animals would obviously be able to walk untiringly for hours through the deep snow.

'The village is only a mile away,' Serge said, pointing with his whip. 'The forest and the sawmill lie beyond. I have business there so I'll leave you to wander around and join you for a meal later. The tavern is over there.'

He pointed to a long hut from the chimney of which smoke rose up into the clear air. They were approaching the village and she looked ahead eagerly. This was no staid English village but a cluster of wooden buildings set higgledy-piggledy around a large spired church. There were some open sheds where she glimpsed ponies and goats tethered and chickens fluttered about the legs of the ponies as they drew rein.

'My uncle is in the cemetery yonder if you wish to make a pilgrimage,' he said.

157

'The villagers won't interfere with you in any way. They have been told we have a visitor from England.'

He dismounted, helped her down and mounted again, raised his hand in a brief farewell and trotted off towards the forest. There was an abruptness in his gestures that irritated her but after a while she realised there was a subtle tactfulness in his apparently high-handed manner. She was free to go where she chose and not bound to make polite comments about what she saw.

A squat little man came up and took the reins of the pony, smiling and gesturing towards the sheds. She couldn't understand a word he said but it was clear that he was offering to stable the pony. She smiled back and nodded to show that she understood and began to walk slowly down the street. One or two doors were open and a plump woman with a kerchief over her head smiled at her, putting her hand to her mouth in shy friendliness. Kate went on, passed some small children playing with a big yellow dog, and turned in at the iron gates of the cemetery. The graves were white mounds of snow with crosses to mark their heads but the names on them were cut in Russian characters and impossible to read. She walked slowly along the indented paths, surmising that the Narodny tomb must be the largest and most imposing, and came upon it abruptly, a great vault of stone guarded by two cherubim and flanked by tall pines. The names were cut in Russian here too and she stared at them in frustration.

There was a crunching noise in the snow and she turned to watch a tall child, muffled in furs, advance within a few feet of her and pause uncertainly; Kate smiled, pointing to the tomb, asking loudly:

'Narodny?'

'Narodny.' The lad took another step forward and said to her in thick-accented French, 'You are visiting with the Narodnys?'

'I am Kate Rye, from England.'

'Mademoiselle Rye.' The boy gave an odd, courtly little bow. 'I am Igor Kerinsky.'

'Kerinsky! Oh, but surely—' Kate's protest trailed away. Clearly this was some younger member of the family, named after his relative. She wondered why anyone should have been named after a thief.

The tomb with its list of incomprehensible names chilled her a little. It was hard to picture the father whom she had never seen as a young man intent on his books and having a secret romance with the English governess. She could picture him only as a heap of bones mouldering among all the other bones in the cold stone vault. Shivering she turned away and met the child's dark eyes fixed on her unwaveringly.

'Where do you live?' she asked. He pointed vaguely towards the huddle of houses and opened his mouth to answer but another voice called, shrilling through the thin, sparkling air.

'Igor! Igor! *Igor!*'

The woman was shouting for him. Kate glimpsed her shawled figure and then the boy ducked away and obeyed the summons, running like a deer over the snow. Kate followed him, calling as she went, in French:

'Good-day to you! My name is—'

The woman must have heard but she gave no sign of having understood. Before the sentence was completed the woman had whirled about and was dragging the child after her, scolding in Russian if Kate had judged her irate tones correctly.

The cemetery looked suddenly unbearably bleak. Kate pulled the wolfskin more closely round her shoulders and went briskly towards the spired church. It was open but deserted, only a red sanctuary lamp burning by the high altar. She paced slowly up the aisle between the rough-hewn stools and benches to the glittering candlesticks. The faint scent of incense still lingered in the air. After the bleak, impoverished appearance of the houses the richness displayed on the altar was a great contrast. These beautiful things must be worth as much as one of the local families could earn in a year, yet they were laid here without guards or locks. Kate marvelled a little at such honesty, or was it fear that left these treasures inviolate?

The door near the altar led, she supposed, into the sacristy. Some movement within the dark alcove caught her eye and she stepped back nervously as a man emerged and peered at her.

He was of indeterminate age, bearded and unkempt with long hair straggling over his shoulders. His clothes were a mixture of skins and woollen shawls tied about him with string but his deep-set eyes were piercingly intelligent.

To her astonishment he spoke in slow, heavily accented English.

'Your name, please? Is it Rye? Is your name Rye?'

'Kate Rye,' she nodded.

'Miss Anne Rye was your mother?'

'Yes, yes, she was.'

'She told me, "One day I or my child will return for what is ours. One day when the danger is past." '

'What?' Kate stared at him.

'Anne Rye,' the stranger repeated. 'You are her child?'

'Yes. I'm Kate Rye. Are you saying that you knew my mother?'

'She has died then?' he asked.

'Four years ago. What danger? Why did she plan to return?'

'She said to me, "One day, when my child is grown and I am strong to face them, I will return." '

'What danger?' she began but the main door was creaking open.

'Tonight or tomorrow,' he hissed, lowering his voice. 'In the chapel at Narodnia. You come and I will give.'

'Give what?' she began but he had

melted into the darkness of the doorway like a shadow.

The main door banged shut and Serge walked down the aisle towards her. 'This meeting in churches is becoming a habit,' he observed. 'By rights I should be waiting by the altar and you should be floating towards me in a white dress. To whom were you talking just now?'

'To whom does one really talk in church?' she countered.

'Touché! Have you found the family mausoleum yet?'

'Mausoleum is right,' she said gravely. 'I couldn't sense anything of him there at all.'

'Because there is nothing. I was never one for relics.'

'You're probably right,' she said and wondered why she had refrained from telling him about the stranger.

'That uncharacteristic meekness tells me that you need feeding up to restore your strength,' he teased. 'Come! I'll take you over to the tavern and buy you piping hot borscht and grilled trout. The menu is limited but ample.'

'I shall grow as fat as a pig,' she complained.

'We Russians like our women firm-fleshed.'

He genuflected briefly to the altar and took her arm as they walked away.

'The priest is away for two or three days visiting relatives,' he said, 'otherwise you would have met him and he would have taken great pride in showing off his few words of English.'

'Is he an old man?' she asked.

'Quite young and exceedingly ambitious,' Serge told her. 'Secretary to a bishop in Moscow is his ultimate aim but his superiors considered he needed experience of the country parish first.'

They had emerged into the cold bright world and crunched across the snow towards the long, low hut with smoke belching from its chimney.

Inside, two steps led down into a warm and smoky interior, furnished with trestle-tables and benches. A huge fire roared up a copper-hooded fireplace in the centre of the room and several men, their furs loosened, were drinking vodka in one corner.

'There is not much work to do this time of the year,' Serge said, guiding her to an empty table. 'In the spring the sowing and planting can begin and when the thaw is here and the river in full flood we can float the cut logs downstream. The winter slows everything.'

'If you made furniture here it would create work, wouldn't it?' Kate said.

'The young men wouldn't drift to the cities in search of employment,' he nodded. 'But you mount me on my hobby-horse again and it is of you I wish to speak. First we will order.' He raised his hands, calling across to a stout woman bent over a cooking stove at the far end of the hut, 'Hey, Marie Fedrovna! Stras vitye? Kak dyela?'

The woman came over, answering in Russian, her manner respectful but not servile. In a very few minutes bowls of the steaming borscht and a pile of crusty fresh-baked rolls were placed before them.

'Cheap but nourishing,' Serge said. 'Marie Fedrovna was widowed when she was quite young but she's worked hard to keep this tavern open and I make a point of eating here once or twice a week. Sometimes she gets a fur-trapper passing through and the local men use the place as a kind of club. Do you like your borscht?'

'It's delicious,' she said truthfully and he nodded, raising his glass of vodka to her as he said, 'Nazdorovye!'

The plump trout and the cabbage flavoured with nutmeg that followed were equally delicious. Kate found herself eating heartily. When she raised her eyes it was to find Serge's brilliant blue eyes fixed on her.

'So you like Narodnia,' he said.

'Very much. It felt like coming home,' she said. 'Oh, you may smile if you choose. I know that's a sentimental thing to say.'

'We Russians are the most sentimental race on earth,' he said. 'We know that it is possible to be homesick for a land one has never seen.'

'And you are being much nicer to me,' she said bluntly.

'Perhaps because I am falling in love with you,' he said.

There was a mocking curl to his straight mouth and she answered lightly. 'Oh, I believe Anna would have something to say about that.'

'Anna cares as little for me as I do for her,' he said. 'Her parents were friends of my father's and Anna their only child. When they were killed in the rail crash she

166

was brought to Narodnia and my aunt took a fancy to her.'

'Aunt Natalya ought to be married,' Kate said.

'She is—to Narodnia and the family,' he said. 'My grandfather, *our* grandfather, was a tyrant. Neither my father nor Aunt Natalya will have it so, of course, but I was a lad of thirteen when he died and I've no very happy memories of the old man. Mind, I think your father's death hit him hard. As far as I can gather Boris was the favourite son, the studious one who might end up as an archbishop.'

'Then he'd not have welcomed the thought of him marrying an English-woman.'

'He'd have hated it,' Serge said flatly. 'Your mother was governess and paid employee. None of the family would have considered her as a possible bride.'

'She came from a respectable family,' Kate began coldly and then smiled as her cousin exclaimed:

'Don't blame me for my grandfather's faults. Remember he was born in the year of Waterloo when serfs were listed as cattle among a rich man's properties. Did you know that serfs were trained to

167

speak with their hands before their mouths so that they wouldn't foul the air for their betters?'

'That's dreadful!' she exclaimed.

'No more dreadful than putting small children down the mines or up chimneys,' he said. 'The world is changing, Katinka, and we must change with it.'

'You're making political speeches again,' she said.

'And beginning to weary you. Finish your meal and we'll ride back slowly.'

'Would it be safe for me to ride alone?' she asked.

'Within reason, if you don't come further than the village. There are markers, of course, for travellers but it's not wise to go further afield. Nina, the pony you're on today, is a reliable little beast and heads for her feedbag when darkness falls so you'll not be able to go far enough to get lost.'

'Will you tell the woman Marie that the meal was marvellous?' she said.

'With pleasure.' He beckoned the woman and spoke to her rapidly in Russian. The woman nodded, smiling at Kate in a friendly fashion.

'I wish I could speak Russian,' Kate said. 'It would be nice to be able to talk to people. Some of them might have known my father or remembered my mother.'

'It takes more than a visit in which to learn our language,' he said, helping her on with her fur cloak as they rose from the table.

A sudden longing that he would ask her to stay for ever rose up in her. It was so strong that she feared he must have read it in her eyes for a little frown came into his own and he said brusquely, 'Time we were getting back to the house.'

As they remounted she caught a glimpse of the tall child and raised an arm in greeting but he ducked away behind a building, averting his head shyly.

'He spoke to me earlier when I was looking at the tomb,' she explained to Serge, 'but a woman called him away.'

'I'm not surprised. The Kerinskys have little affection for the Narodnys or their guests,' he said.

'Because of the man who was hanged?'

'You've heard about that?' He looked faintly surprised.

'Babushka mentioned it and Aunt Natalya told me a servant called Igor Kerinsky was hanged for stealing some money.'

'It was an unpleasant business,' Serge

said. 'I was only a small child at the time. In fact we were living in St Petersburg —Peter had just been born and we hadn't yet returned to Narodnia. Kerinsky was a trusted servant. He helped my grandfather with the accounts and made purchases on his behalf. Apparently he helped himself to some of Babushka's jewels at the same time. Their loss was reported and they were found in his room. His family has maintained ever since that he was innocent, of course.'

'And what did he say himself?' she asked.

'I believe he confessed. I don't remember anything about it at the actual time but occasionally when Babushka is confused or upset she will mention him. It must have upset her to meet you, of course.'

'I didn't want to upset her,' she said defensively.

'Of course not, but one cannot be certain with Babushka. She has been vague and timid ever since I can remember. You mustn't mind,' he said.

'I hoped—I wanted her to like me,' she said.

'Because you're Boris's daughter?' He slanted her an ironic smile and said,

'You really are Russian, aren't you! Full of sentiment that you try to hide under that cool schoolmarm exterior.'

Kate flushed uncomfortably. It was unnerving to be so accurately assessed and she guessed too that he was laughing at her.

When they reached the house he helped her down and held her for a moment, looking down into her face.

'What I said in church I meant,' he said. 'I am falling in love with you.'

'Which is very foolish,' she said lightly, 'for the Narodny family would never countenance marriage to a bastard.'

'I am not the entire Narodny family,' he said. 'I am one member of it, Katinka, and I make up my own mind.'

'As I do!' She slipped from his grasp and went indoors, her cheeks pink with more than the cold.

Anna was arranging some dried grasses in a tall vase on the table in the inner hall. She acknowledged Kate with a tight little smile but something in her face told the other that through the open doors she had glimpsed Serge and Kate standing so close together.

Kate went upstairs without speaking

and gained her room without too much difficulty. The wolfskin cloak was still around her shoulders and she took it off slowly, feeling the warmth of it about her as if Serge's hands still touched it.

He had said that he was beginning to fall in love with her and she was inclined to believe him but her own feelings troubled her. She had never known any young man intimately and so had no basis for comparison but when Serge kissed her or touched her or even looked at her she felt a tumultuous excitement, an impatience with her settled, dull existence and a longing for something wild and free that beat in her blood and was the most potent legacy from her father.

But Serge, whether he wanted it or not, was expected to marry Anna Nicholaevna. Only in novels did the hero flout convention and marry the poor heroine. Even her own father, for all his gentleness—Kate bit her lip and decided she would stop thinking about her possible marriage with Serge. There were still questions to be answered and she hoped the strange ragged man would get to the chapel that night and answer the queries she had.

To her disappointment, when she went

down to the dining-room for the evening meal, Serge was not there. Peter, coming forward to greet her, said, 'My brother has taken himself off for the night to carouse with his friends, so you will have to put up with me to entertain you.'

'Which I shall enjoy very much.'

She smiled up at him, thinking what an attractive young man he was. It was amusing to flirt with him a little and as the meal progressed she began to flatter herself that despite her inexperience she was able to hold a man's attention. It was a pity Serge was not here so that she could tease him a little by devoting her conversation to his brother.

'You are in a good humour,' her uncle observed, smiling a trifle sourly as she finished a lively account of a Parents' Day meeting at which two of the smaller pupils had let loose a pet mouse.

'She was with Serge this afternoon,' Anna said, an edge to her voice.

'We rode into the village and I had a look at the church there,' Kate said, 'but the priest was away.'

'Visiting relatives,' Aunt Natalya said, and nodded.

'He is a very bright young man,' the

Count said. 'We used to have our own priest, you know, but he left us very abruptly. It would have been round about the time that Boris died. Just before if I recall rightly. He left word that he had had a revelation and intended to become a *starets*. That's a kind of wandering prophet, Kate. There are many such holy men in Russia and some of them have great influence.'

'We have no family priest and no services in our chapel since poor Boris died,' Aunt Natalya said. 'For my own part I never liked Father Fyodor very much. He came from a poor family and my father advanced him rapidly. In my opinion he showed gross ingratitude.'

Two deaths—three, if one counted the hanging of Igor Kerinsky, and two disappearances within a year. That had been a strange and tragic period in the life of the respectable Narodny family, Kate thought.

The meal over they retired to the drawing-room. Kate was pleased when Anna sat down at the pianoforte at Aunt Natalya's request and began to play in a correct but rather lifeless manner.

At the first opportunity she slipped from

the apartment, murmuring an excuse about fetching a shawl, and made her way back through the long passages to the chapel. The candles still burned here and the red sanctuary lamp glowed brightly but the place was deserted. She went in and wandered slowly round, wondering if she had chosen the wrong time of the evening or if the stranger would come to keep the appointment.

Surely the man in the church must be the family priest who had left in order to became a *starets*. Some very urgent revelation must have led him to take such a drastic step. Kate doubted if the revelation had been a religious one. It was more likely to have been some dangerous knowledge that had been entrusted to him.

The theft of Babushka's jewels, the arrest and execution of Igor Kerinksy, Boris's skating accident, her mother's flight back to England, even Olga's death—all those events rushed together in her mind.

The door creaked open and she swung round, her nerves tingling.

'Mademoiselle, is everything all right?'

Marisa, black-gowned and erect, entered the chapel, her face a pale blur in the shadow.

175

'Perfectly all right,' Kate said sharply. 'Why shouldn't it be?'

'No reason, Mademoiselle, but the chapel is cold and you neglected to fetch your shawl,' the housekeeper said expressionlessly.

'It's peaccful here,' Kate said. 'I have every right to come in, you know.'

'Of course, Mademoiselle.' Marisa had turned and was holding the door open.

If Kate stayed longer the *starets* might interrupt them both. Inwardly fuming, she went through into the passage again.

'Your room is comfortable, I hope?' the housekeeper said.

'Yes, very comfortable. I like Narodnia very much,' Kate said with a little touch of defiance.

'Mademoiselle, it would be better if you returned very soon to England,' Marisa said. She spoke in a low tone staring straight ahead of her as they walked along the corridor.

'Why? What do you mean?' Kate began.

'Nothing, Mademoiselle. I only say that it would be better for you to leave.'

Before Kate could question her further the other had turned and gone swiftly up the stairs.

NINE

'We must have a party for you, Kate,' Aunt Natalya said the next morning. 'A real old-fashioned party with music and games and gifts for the village children. We haven't had one of those for ages.'

'There will be very few to come,' the Count said. 'Most of our neighbours are still in St Petersburg.'

'The Scholtskis and the Ivanovs are back,' Peter said. 'They'd be glad of an excuse for celebration and the advent of a beautiful relative from England is surely sufficient reason.'

'If the circumstances were only different,' the Count murmured. Kate knew he referred to her bastardy and flushed angrily but it was Serge who answered his father, his voice impatient.

'Isn't it time we really moved forward a little? Kate cannot enjoy being regarded as a blot on the family honour.'

'Personally I'm tired of hearing about the saintly virtues of poor Uncle Boris,'

Peter murmured. 'It's quite a relief to discover he was capable of falling in love.'

'With the governess,' Anna said, her eyes contemptuous.

'Well, we cannot have a party during Lent,' the Count said, 'but when the thaw comes, after Holy Saturday, I see no reason why we shouldn't celebrate Easter in the old fashion. What do you plan to do with yourself today, Kate?'

'I shall ride out and do a little exploring,' Kate said.

'I'll come with you,' Peter offered.

'No, I'd really like to go alone,' she said hastily.

If she rode to the village there was the chance of meeting the *starets* again and learning more of his message. She hadn't returned to the chapel the previous night and had no idea whether he had tried to keep the appointment.

'Don't go too far. The weather looks a little uncertain,' Serge said as they rose from what had been an early lunch.

'And have a hot drink before you set out, to fortify yourself against the cold,' Aunt Natalya said, fussily.

Kate succeeded in extricating herself from the torrent of well meant advice and went upstairs to put on her outdoor garments. She was beginning to find her way round the main family apartments but had decided to postpone further exploration of the mansion until a day came when the weather forced her to remain indoors.

Marisa was in the bedroom, obviously checking to see that the maids had done their work properly, and she went out as Kate entered, giving the girl a brief curtsey and a mumbled 'Good-morning'. It would have been a waste of time to ask her what she had meant by her warning of the previous day for her face was tightly closed against intrusion.

The samovar was bubbling merrily in the corner. Kate poured herself a cup of the strong fragrant tea and sipped it thoughtfully, wondering yet again what danger could lurk under the quiet, respectable façade of this remote community. No doubt the *starets* would tell her when they met again.

Nina was already saddled at the main door and Anton helped her to mount. Her intention of going to the village weakened when she glanced up at the sky. Heavy white clouds were scudding across it and a metallic streak above the

179

horizon threatened a storm. The wind had freshened, blowing eddies of snow into her face. It would be wiser, she decided, to confine herself to ride near the house. She set off at a walk, bending her head into the wind and hunching over her saddle.

The land beyond the other side of the house dipped and rose between scattered pine trees. There had been no attempt to make any kind of formal gardens but the monotony of the landscape was broken by long rows of thorn bushes, black lace above the white snow. Nina trotted steadily forward, surefooted even in the deepest drift. A few minutes more and a curtain of blowing snow rose between her and the high walls of Narodnia.

She rode on, her head drooping a little. The whiteness filling the air, the steady jogging motion of the pony, the humming of the wind through the pines were combining into an unreality that was almost like a dream. Her eyes were closing and there was a queer, sweetish taste in her mouth.

It was dangerous to sleep in the snow. She had read that somewhere and she tried to open her eyes and sit up straight but her muscles felt like lead and behind her lowered eyelids the vague images shimmered into blackness. There was a sudden whirling sensation and she was falling down into darkness. Something cold hit her sharply in the face and she scrambled up to her knees, spitting out a mouthful of icy snow. Nina stood a few paces away, regarding her erstwhile rider with a slightly cynical curl of the lips.

Kate was awake but her legs felt curiously weak and her eyes were blurred with an overmastering desire to sleep again. If she gave into it she might never get up again. Already her hands and feet were growing numb and an overpowering lethargy shackled her.

Into her mind came a vivid image of Marisa hurrying from the bedroom, of herself sipping the strongly flavoured tea.

If she went back to the house in her present state there was the danger of finding herself alone with no means of defence against an enemy. Better to find somewhere she could sleep off the effects of whatever had caused her to sleep and then ride back when her mind was alert again.

With a great effort she struggled up to the saddle again, her legs shaking as

181

she mounted clumsily. Nina seemed to understand for she gave little whinnies of encouragement as Kate pulled herself up to the saddle and clung there. The snow mist was thicker now but the pony walked forward again as if she knew exactly where she was going, so Kate let her have her head and concentrated desperately on keeping her seat as they moved further into the trees.

The wooden hut loomed up suddenly, its walls of split logs reassuringly solid. She made her way slowly up to the door and half fell against it. It gave way easily, swinging inward, and she led Nina within and pushed the door shut behind them both.

The interior was piled with hay and a tiny window afforded a faint light. The hay was dry, soft and warm but the exhaustion had finally caught up with her and it would have made no difference if she had seen wet straw. Her last conscious thought as she sank down into the hay was that, danger or no danger, she would stay at Narodnia until she had ferreted out its secrets.

She woke to darkness and the howling of wind outside the hut. Nina, cheated of her feedbag, had begun to make a meal of the hay. Kate felt better apart from a nagging headache and an intense thirst. She was certain something had been given to her to make her sleep and it could only have been put into the tea. As far as she could recall they had all eaten and drunk the same things at lunchtime. It would have been so easy for her to lie down and freeze to death if the drug had been a little stronger or she had drunk more of the tea.

As it was she was obviously trapped here until morning. The pane of glass in the tiny window revealed nothing but swirling snow and far off she discerned a sound that cut through the howling of the wind on a different note. The hair at the back of her neck prickled with fear. She had never heard the crying of wolves through the snow before but she sensed the sound now and any notion she had entertained of trying to make her way back to the house vanished. She would stay here until either morning or help came. She pulled the cloak more tightly about herself and looked wryly at Nina happily munching her straw.

Someone at Narodnia wanted to drive

her away from the place. Marisa had made it plain that it would be better for her to leave. Anna had made it equally clear that she disliked her. Kate wondered if it was a jealous fear that she might usurp the place Anna had carved out for herself in the affections of Babushka and Aunt Natalya, or did Anna secretly dislike the attention Serge was paying her? And what of the Count, the uncle who had been so reluctant to welcome her? Had it been dislike of scandal or something darker that lay in the past?

Two brothers, a year apart in age, but different in temperament. Boris had been the devout, studious one, apparently wedded to his books while Alexis was already married with two small children. If Boris had died unwed, the two children would double their share of the inheritance. Murder had been committed for much less than that.

'And now my imagination is really running away with me,' Kate said aloud. 'My father skated out on the ice and was drowned and my mother rushed back to England in a state of grief and shock.'

Telling the family priest she would return when the danger was past. Anne Rye had borne her illegitimate child, intending to reveal the truth of her birth when Kate came of age. She had not really expected to die only seventeen years later, leaving only the bare facts for her daughter to read in a lawyer's letter.

Kate paced up and down the hut. Her eyes were becoming accustomed to the darkness and there was something queerly reassuring about the pony's chunky little shape as she munched the hay. The howling of wind and wolves had grown to a deafening pitch and dropped away into a white silence. She was becoming more hungry and more thirsty with every moment that passed and the hut, refuge though it had been, was neither warm nor comfortable. Kate squinted at her fob-watch but it was too dark to distinguish the position of the hands and she suspected that her tumble into the snow had stopped it anyway.

There were other sounds beyond the hut. She raised her head, trying to identify them. Cries, muffled by the falling snow, reached her straining ears and through the glass she saw pinpricks of light diffused by the whiteness.

Stumbling over a bale of hay, Kate made

her way to the door and tugged it open, waving her arm and shouting into the falling snow. The shouts were growing louder, the pinpoints of light flaring into torches. A ragged line of dark shapes was advancing towards her and she shouted again and she felt her voice caught up in the wind and tossed aside.

One of the figures quickened its pace and she closed her eyes in brief thankfulness as Serge dismounted and pulled her roughly into his arms.

'What the hell happened?' he demanded. His angry voice was the most welcome thing she had heard for hours and she leaned against the protective bulk of his thick cloak and jerkin.

'What possessed you to ride so far and in this direction? It's nowhere near the village!' he exclaimed.

'I didn't mean to go so far and then the snow came,' she said meekly.

She had no intention of voicing her suspicions that she had been given some kind of sleeping draught. It would have sounded completely hysterical and as yet she had no proof.

'You've not got the sense of a kitten!' he was scolding. 'You might have frozen to death and not been discovered for days.'

'You took long enough to come seeking!' she retorted.

'Anna declared she'd seen you return, so we wasted time searching the house, and then we rode over to the village but nobody had seen you there either. After that we had to organise a full search.'

He raised his arm, shouting to the approaching riders. Kate heard whatever he had said being repeated down the line and the flaming torches were waved to and fro.

'I didn't return, so Anna couldn't have seen me,' Kate began but Serge was leading Nina out, helping Kate up to the mare's broad back.

'We'll ride back,' he said, mounting up himself and leaning to take Nina's reins. 'Can you stay on without falling off?'

'Of course I can,' she began and asked with sudden curiosity. 'How did you know I fell off before?'

'Because you're a helpless female!' he shouted as they rode into the teeth of the wind that seemed to spring up from nowhere as if to remind them that violence was not yet done.

The other searchers closed in behind

them. Kate heard them calling to one another in the language she wished passionately she could understand. Then Serge tugged on Nina's rein and the pony quickened her steps with a high whinnying of protest. No doubt after her good meal of hay she was in no mood to carry a rider again but, being an amiable little lady, permitted herself only a slight token of displeasure.

Lights blazed from the windows and front door of the house and Peter came galloping from the other direction, a beaver hat pulled down to his eyebrows.

'The wanderer is returned,' Serge announced, dismounting and lifting her down.

'Thank the Lord!' Peter had leapt down and was hugging her with what seemed like genuine pleasure.

Kate wished that she could have frozen time for just a few seconds so that she could have seen those first unguarded reactions before their faces broke into smiles and their voices surged about her as she was helped into the hall. There was too much noise and bustle, too many voices exclaiming and marvelling for her to have a clear picture of any of it.

'My dear, you must be chilled to the bone!' She was enfolded in Aunt Natalya's warm embrace. 'You ought to have told someone where you were riding. Serge, where did you find her?'

'In the old hay-hut beyond the eastern furrow.'

'It was a miracle she chanced upon the place.' This from Peter, who kept hugging her as if she had been missing for years.

'Anna said she had seen you come back,' her uncle said.

'I was mistaken,' Anna said. Her small face was expressionless, her hands plucking her skirt nervously.

'How could you have been?' Aunt Natalya said. 'It doesn't make sense, my love. Either you saw Kate ride back or you did not!'

'It must have been one of the servants,' Anna said.

'It was a foolish mistake and might have cost a life,' the Count said, sternly.

Anna flushed and bit her lip, her fingers plucking more urgently at her dress, her eyes full of disappointment she was too inexperienced to hide. Was the disappointment because she had genuinely made a mistake or because her lie had not worked, or had she been the one to slip something into the tea?

'A hot drink for everybody!' Aunt Natalya clapped her hands imperiously. 'Kate! You must get out of those wet garments at once. Upstairs with you now, and then you must have your supper by the fire in the drawing-room and tell us all your adventures. I tell you I have been out of my mind with anxiety. Positively out of my mind! We ought not to have let you ride so far alone!'

'I won't be long.'

Kate left them still talking in the hall and went upstairs. Reaction was setting in and she felt cold and shivery.

Marisa was in the bedroom, laying out a robe and slippers. She had evidently heard the bustle of arrival and now was filling her duties as perfect housekeeper. Her face expressed neither regret nor pleasure as she turned.

'So you were found, Mademoiselle? I am pleased.'

'Are you?' Kate began to pull off her garments. They were sodden with the snow and her hair had begun to come down and hung in little rat's tails about her face. Serge must have seen her like this, she

190

realised, and felt a pang of exasperation.

'But of course, Mademoiselle. It is very dangerous to be lost in the snow,' Marisa said calmly.

'Not really lost. I took shelter,' Kate said. 'I seem to have missed my supper.'

'The others ate as they came and went,' Marisa said, making it sound as if it were Kate's fault that the arrangements for the evening meal had been upset.

'What time is it?' Kate reached for the high-collared robe, wrapping it about herself snugly.

'Past eight o'clock, Mademoiselle.'

'Is that all? I thought it was the middle of the night.' Kate pulled the remaining pins out of her hair and sat down at the dressing-table. Marisa had picked up the brush and began now to use it, expertly and soothingly, on the tangled brown mass falling down Kate's back.

'I shall be glad of something to eat.' Kate spoke lazily, her eyes on the mirror. 'I had some tea before I went out but I don't suppose there's any left now?'

Marisa's eyes had flicked towards the samovar, now mute and empty in the corner, but she answered with perfect composure:

191

'I will have fresh tea brewed for you, Mademoiselle.'

'Do you always make the tea?' Kate asked.

'For the family, yes. They drink a finer blend than is served to the rest of the household.'

She sounded completely unconcerned, her hand unfaltering as it wielded the brush. Had it been only imagination born of panic that had given Kate the conviction her sleepiness had been induced? It was possible to be mistaken especially when one had recently travelled a long distance through unfamiliar country. Kate remembered the numbness in her hands and feet, the blurring of her vision.

'I have been feeling quite tired,' she said abruptly, 'but it's hard to sleep. I wonder if you could suggest something?'

'To help you sleep?' Marisa raised her eyebrows in faint surprise.

'Surely people in Russia need a mild sleeping draught occasionally,' Kate said.

Again the housekeeper's eyes flickered towards the empty samovar but she said, as if considering the matter, 'I believe years ago, Madame Olga had need of some laudanum when she was feverish.

No doubt I could find it but after so many years I doubt if it would be much use.'

She had plaited Kate's hair loosely and now coiled it round at the back of her head. Her whole attention seemed concentrated on the task.

'I'll go downstairs again,' Kate said, rising from the mirror. 'I must thank my rescuers and find out how Anna could have made such a foolish mistake. The search for me was delayed, you know, because she thought she had seen me returning.'

'In the snow it's easy to be mistaken,' Marisa said impassively.

Kate gave her a long level look and marched out. There were still people talking in the hall. She guessed that the afternoon events would be an excuse for much boasting and self-congratulations. The loss of anyone in the snow would provide a kind of grisly excitement in the bleak placidity of their lives.

A small table had been set by the fire in the drawing-room and Serge waved her to an armchair as she entered. He had taken off his snow-covered garments and wore the customary high-necked tunic and baggy trousers but the afternoon's events had served to stimulate rather than exhaust him. His eyes were a blazing blue in the lean brown planes of his face, his voice teasing as he said, 'Come and have some real food, pretty Cousin. Snow and straw are not the best diet for a gently reared young lady!'

'I believe you missed your own supper,' she began.

'Not me, Katinka! I sat down and had a good meal before I joined the search,' he said unfeelingly. 'It was Peter who went dashing off to rescue the fair maiden! You have made a decided impression upon my susceptible younger brother.'

'Then my visit hasn't been in vain,' she said flippantly. 'Good-evening, Aunt Natalya. I'm so sorry to have caused so much trouble.'

Her aunt, who had just come in with Anna at her heels, waved her small hands deprecatingly.

'I blame myself. This is treacherous country even when one lives here. For my own part I seldom stir except when we go to St Petersburg of course.'

'Where I will have to go in a week or two,' Serge said, helping himself to an apple from Kate's supper table.

'My dear boy, you've only just come

home again!' Aunt Natalya exclaimed.

'Oh, I won't be away above a couple of weeks. We've an export order for some of the spruce-firs and I'm due back in the city to sign the order on father's behalf. Why don't you come with me, Katinka?'

He turned, a questioning smile on his lips, but there was something else in his face. Something hard and ruthless flashed in the smiling blue eyes and was instantly gone.

'I absolutely refuse to let you drag poor Kate all that way just so you can bore her to death with business talk,' Aunt Natalya said. 'I want to plan the party we are to have. I think we really do have something to celebrate now!'

Anna made an abrupt little movement as if she were protesting silently against the fuss being lavished on this foreign interloper.

Kate turned to her, her brown eyes sparkling with irritation:

'I hope you agree, Anna,' she said silkily. 'You would have felt so bad if your mistake had resulted in my being frozen to death out in the snow.'

'First nearly burnt to a crisp and then frozen,' Peter said, coming in. 'You lead an exciting life, Kate.'

'I do hope we have seen the last of all the excitement,' Aunt Natalya said with a nervous little giggle.

'Oh, I shall take very good care of myself in future,' Kate said, her eyes still fixed on Anna.

'You will have me as your stalwart protector,' Peter said. 'Serge may go rushing off to St Petersburg if he chooses but I shall stay here. Narodnia suddenly seems more attractive than it's ever been before.'

It was flattering to be admired by such a personable young man but she felt a sense of disappointment at Serge's proposed absence. Surely he could have completed his business dealings before coming to Narodnia. She decided that the last thing she would do would be to betray her feelings, so kept her gaze turned from him resolutely and favoured her younger cousin with a long, sweeping glance from beneath her eyelashes.

'Serge! Peter!'

The Count was calling his sons sharply from the hall. They rose in a leisurely manner but the summons was repeated more urgently. There was a babble of voices in the hall and Aunt Natalya, her face puzzled and concerned, stood up, one hand spread for quietness.

'What is it?' Anna asked.

'I am not certain. Something seems to be wrong.' Aunt Natalya moved towards the door just as the Count came in, his heavy face drawn into sombre lines.

'Some of the moujiks were still searching, not knowing that Kate had been found,' he said, 'and they came across a body in the snow.'

'Whose body?' Anna asked sharply.

'Natalya, it's our old priest,' the Count said.

'The one who left to become a *starets?*' Anna said.

'Father Fyodor,' her guardian nodded. 'It's more than twenty years since we saw him but I'll swear he's the same man. He was apparently on his way here. Jannski says the body was only about a hundred yards from the chapel door.'

'But how—what happened?' Aunt Natalya said.

'It looks as if he lost his footing and hit his head on the ice,' he said. 'I've told the men to put his body in the chapel for tonight and we'll ride over to the village tomorrow to make arrangements for the burial. This is a sad affair. He must have been coming to visit us, after all these years! A sad affair!'

Sadder than you know, Kate thought bleakly. The *starets* would keep the appointment in the chapel after all but he was in no state to deliver his message.

TEN

The next day there was the feeling of disaster in the air. Kate could think of no other way to describe the queer uneasiness that seemed to pervade the great house. The servants were congregated in groups of three or four, whispering together as she passed them in the long corridor, and even Aunt Natalya seemed nervous, two spots of high colour on her cheekbones as she talked quickly and jerkily.

'I cannot believe it! Poor Father Fyodor has been away for so many years that we had come to the conclusion he must have died. I wonder how long he had been in the district. He must have stayed somewhere, perhaps in the church, with our own priest being away. And to set out on foot in such a blizzard!'

'And to slip on the ice and fall,' Kate said. 'Aunt Natalya, under what circumstances did he leave Narodnia? You said it was round about the time my father died.'

'Just before—no, a day or so later, if I remember it rightly.' The older woman wrinkled her forehead, her eyes clouding. 'Yes, it was afterwards. Father was very angry because we had to send for a priest to offer Mass for the recovery of Boris's body and to give poor Olga the last rites. We had word later that Father Fyodor had gone off on the spur of the moment to become a *starets*.'

'He might have chosen a more convenient time for his revelation,' Serge said.

He had just ridden back from the village and looked grim and dour, his face set in hard lines.

'One cannot question the ways of God,' his aunt said gently.

'His body will be taken to the village and buried in the churchyard there,' Serge said. 'Peter and I will attend with Father as representatives of the family. Has Babushka been told?'

'I thought it best not to say anything,' Aunt Natalya said. 'She has a slight chill anyway, so it's not a good idea to upset the poor soul.'

'It's not serious, is it?' Kate asked sharply.

'No, merely a chill but at her age one doesn't want to give her bad news. Oh, dear, we will have to postpone the party now, I suppose. One must show some respect.'

'As he left the place more than twenty years ago, I really don't think we need go into full mourning as if we'd just lost a member of the family,' Peter objected. 'Anyway I'm looking forward very much to dancing with my pretty cousin again.'

'I think Aunt Natalya is right,' Serge said. 'We should delay any social junketings for at least a month.'

'In that case I shall go to St Petersburg with you,' Peter said.

'I knew you wouldn't stay long at home,' Serge said with a resigned look.

'Perhaps I shall buy some jewels for a pretty lady,' the young man said, his eyes teasing.

Kate had a tremor of apprehension. Surely Peter had not taken her friendly manner towards him as a sign that she was falling in love! She had assumed that he had merely been flirting a little with her but now she was not so certain.

'We'll postpone our little entertainment for two weeks then,' Aunt Natalya said. 'At least the blizzard has died down, which is a great relief, but you will be very cautious if you venture out today, won't you, Kate?'

'I think I'll stay in my room by the fire and read,' Kate said. 'Last evening's adventure affected me more than I realised.'

'Very wise of you, my love,' Aunt Natalya said, looking slightly relieved at not having to entertain her guest.

Kate excused herself and went upstairs slowly. Out of some obscure feeling that she ought to show some respect for the memory of the *starets* she put on a dark gown and the dress matched her mood. Two accidents within such a short space of time followed by the death of the *starets* was surely more than a coincidence. It began to look, she thought unhappily, as if someone wanted either to frighten or even kill her and there was, as far as she knew, no reason for anyone to want her death.

On impulse she turned and made her

way into the wing where her grandmother's rooms were situated. It was her right to visit the old lady, she told herself firmly, as she threaded the corridors and came to a wide staircase.

The door at the top was closed but it yielded readily to her touch and she went through to the room where her grandmother had received her before.

The fire was crackling merrily and the thin golden sunshine poured through the windows, giving a cheerful aspect to the cluttered apartment. On her first visit Kate had been too interested in meeting Babushka to have leisure to spare for looking round the room but now her eyes roamed with bewildered amusement about the huge apartment with its tables crammed with ornaments of china and silver, the painted wooden dolls set in a row along one wall, the fans spreading their ivory sticks against dark velvet, the cherub-flanked clock.

'Come to me, Katharina Borisova.' Babushka's voice, a trifle husky but still clear, came from the depths of a wing-backed chair set in the shadowed corner and partly concealed by a painted screen.

Kate went forward and curtsied to the old lady who sat, straight-backed, her white-capped head held high. The brilliant shawl was still about her shoulders and her hand, as she leaned to clasp the younger girl's hand, was encrusted with gems.

'I came to see how you were,' Kate said. 'Aunt Natalya said you had a chill.'

' 'Tis nothing at all,' the old lady said. 'I am glad to see you, child. It is necessary for us to talk.'

'You do know who I am?' Kate said.

'You are the child of my son, Boris, and the English governess who came—many years ago, I cannot tell how many. I get muddled sometimes, my dear.'

'You ought to come down and join the family,' Kate said. 'It must be lonely up here all by yourself.'

'I like to be lonely,' Babushka said, setting her mouth firmly. 'I like the peace and the quiet, but they don't tell me things. They hide things from me, you know.'

'What kind of things?' Kate asked.

'There is death in the house,' Babushka said. 'I hear the servants whispering and then they see me and fall silent. Who is dead? Is it Igor?'

'Igor Kerinsky died a long time ago,' Kate said gently.

'Of course. I told you that I sometimes get confused. He stole some of my jewels and they hanged him for it. That was what they told me anyway. I was very fond of Igor even if his parents were moujiks and I was very unhappy when he betrayed me. I couldn't believe that he was a thief. He had always been so quiet, so polite.'

She had been speaking in French and her voice rose jerkily while she clutched at Kate's hands. Then abruptly her grip slackened and she said, shaking her head to and fro, 'All old tales and best forgotten. Who died in the house?'

She shot the question so swiftly at Kate that the girl answered without having time to think.

'I believe his name was Father Fyodor. He was on his way to visit when he was caught in the storm.'

'Father Fyodor! Why, it must be years since he left us. He was our priest, you know.'

'Yes, I know. I was sorry to hear about it,' Kate said.

'Ah, he was a strange, moody man,' Babushka said. 'He left us very suddenly—

to become a holy man, my husband said. I was never certain that I believed that was the reason. It had something to do with poor Igor's hanging. He was such a pleasant-looking young man. So polite and modest and attentive. Poor Igor!'

Her voice had dropped to a husky murmur and her fine-boned face was sad. She looked up at Kate, frowning a little as if she tried to bring her granddaughter into focus, and said:

'You must go back, my dear. Go back to England. Don't stay here.'

'Why not? Why mustn't I stay?' Kate said.

Babushka was going to answer. Kate was quite certain of that but there was a slight cough from the doorway and Marisa came in. The housekeeper had been hurrying a little. There were beads of moisture along her upper lip and she was breathing rather quickly but her voice had its usual calm timbre as she said:

'Why, Mademoiselle, I didn't realise you were here. We must be careful not to tire Madame Ilsa.'

'She must go back to England,' Babushka said and broke into a flood of Russian. Marisa answered, evidently soothing her, then turned again to Kate.

'She needs to rest now,' she said. 'Please Mademoiselle, have the goodness to come away.'

Babushka had leaned back in her chair, closing her eyes. From the depths of the brilliant shawl she said, 'Go back to England! Don't stay.'

There were so many questions to be asked but Marisa stood there like a silent gaoler. Kate had to turn and with as much dignity as possible retrace her steps through the cluttered room.

At the staircase she paused but it was Marisa who spoke first.

'Madame Ilsa is old and excitement is bad for her. Perhaps you will tell me, Mademoiselle, if you intend to visit her again?'

'She told me to go back to England. Why?' Kate demanded.

'It is better that you should, as your mother did,' Marisa said.

'But why?' Kate began but the housekeeper had gone back into the room, closing the door firmly behind her.

In the passage she hesitated again, wondering whether to keep her word and read for a few hours in the comfort of her room or go back downstairs.

The sound of low voices downstairs from a partly open door along the corridor arrested her attention.

They were speaking French and though many of the words were muffled she caught their sense. First the man's voice, low and intense:

'—dangerous until we can—'

'The Englishwoman—has to—cannot endure.'

That was a female voice, lighter in tone but filled with equal passion.

'Patience,' the man said. 'We must have patience.'

There was a sobbing intake of breath and Kate caught the girl's words.

'Act now—don't you want to? I cannot—'

A maidservant with a pile of linen in her arms was coming up a side staircase. Kate turned and fled in the opposite direction to her room where she sat down heavily.

Peter and Anna? What had those few snatches of conversation meant? She had no difficulty in imagining the sullen Anna capable of intrigue but Peter had seemed to be so open and friendly, so devoid of guile.

Clasping her hands together tightly she

ran through the events in her mind. Twenty-two years before, her mother had come to this house as governess to Aunt Natalya. Her formidable grandfather and his gentle son had been alive then and Uncle Alexis had been living in St Petersburg with his young wife and two small children. And Igor Kerinsky had been a trusted servant.

A trusted servant who had stolen her grandmother's jewels and been hanged for his crime. And then Uncle Alexis had brought his family to Narodnia on a visit and Boris had fallen through the ice and died. That was when her mother had returned to England without giving notice and the family priest had gone off to become a wandering holy man. That was when Olga, her uncle's wife, had died. A tragic sequence of events and running through them a connecting thread that she hadn't been able to grasp.

Her mother had intended to return. She had said so to Father Fyodor and she must have said something at the monastery too—sufficient to alarm the priest when he recognised her daughter more than twenty years later.

Kate listed the people of Narodnia in her

mind. Uncle Alexis hadn't wanted her to come to Russia and accepted her now only grudgingly. Serge too had been suspicious of her motives but was apparently falling in love with her. Only Peter and Aunt Natalya had welcomed their unknown relative and now it looked as if Peter were hatching some sort of scheme with Anna, who had displayed her resentment of Kate quite openly.

The bed-hanging had caught fire. Anyone could have crept in as she slept. Even Serge, much as she hated to believe it, could have set the curtains alight and then pretended to rescue her, either to frighten her away or to divert suspicion from himself when a later, more successful attempt was made.

Anyone could have slipped something into the tea hoping she would drink it and fall asleep while she was out riding alone. Anna had delayed the search by pretending she had seen Kate return but the girl might have been taking advantage of an opportunity that somebody else had made.

If only she could speak Russian she could talk to the villagers, find someone who remembered the events surrounding her father's death. Kate sighed, wondering if even a knowledge of Russian would serve. The people in the district were moujiks, freed only a generation before from centuries of slavery, but still bound to the Narodny family by centuries of loyalty and submission.

It was frustrating to sit, not knowing which avenue to explore. Babushka knew something but she was old and confused and Marisa was evidently determined that Kate would find no further opportunity for talking to her alone.

The evening meal that night was a cheerless affair. The Count was absent, supervising the removal of the *starets's* body to the village church where he would be buried the next day with the men of the family to pay their last respects. Peter was not his usual talkative self and Serge favoured her with no more than a nod and a brief greeting. As soon as possible Kate excused herself and went upstairs again.

It had been a little disconcerting to discover there was neither lock nor bolt on her door but a little reflection served to convince her that she stood in no real danger while she slept. It was apparent accidents she had to fear and nobody would believe that she could set her bedcovers alight twice.

Having reassured herself she closed the door and fell asleep almost at once.

In the morning the three men of the house rode over to the village. Watching them go, Kate felt the now familiar unease grip her. The Count, slumped in his saddle between his two sons, looked more disillusioned with life than ever. No doubt the return and death of Father Fyodor had reminded him of other unhappy days.

'I hate unhappiness,' Aunt Natalya said, coming to her side. 'This should be a happy house. We live too much in the past, I sometimes think. Why, we are practically in the twentieth century and we should not be brooding on far-off unhappy events.'

'Is Babushka well?' Kate asked.

'Better but she's resting today. When spring comes then she'll venture out. I fear we worry about her too much but we have always been a close-knit family. And now you are part of us.'

'I hoped to be,' Kate said.

'Of course you are,' Aunt Natalya took her hand and pressed it warmly. 'You really mustn't take any notice of Anna. She is a dear, good girl but she is a trifle

211

jealous of you. I don't suppose you realise what a pretty girl you are.'

'No, I am not often complimented on my looks,' Kate said wryly.

'Serge and Peter are both immensely taken with you,' her aunt said. 'They think an old spinster doesn't notice these things but I was young once.'

'You're still young,' Kate said.

'Oh, I was admired when I was a girl,' her aunt said, preening herself a trifle. 'They used to call me the beautiful Natalya. But marriage was not to be my portion in life and I cannot honestly say that I regret it. But you must certainly marry, my dear, oh, you and Peter would make such a charming couple.'

'Peter!' Kate couldn't avoid the exclamation of distress.

'I thought you were fond of him,' Aunt Natalya said, looking disappointed. 'Oh, I know it's very soon but I am an inveterate matchmaker.'

'I doubt if Uncle Alexis would take kindly to the idea of either of his sons marrying a bastard,' Kate said bluntly.

'I have great respect for tradition,' Aunt Natalya said, 'but there are some that should be abolished. It is too cruel to

212

punish a child for the wrongdoings of its parents!'

'I'm fond of both my cousins,' Kate said firmly, 'but I've no intention of marrying anybody.'

Her tone was full of conviction but her aunt gave her an archly disbelieving look.

The rest of the day passed slowly. Kate would have liked to ride out but her aunt seemed to crave her company and, with Anna presumably closeted with Babushka, she felt obliged to sit chatting by the fire.

'When Serge and Anna are married,' was her almost invariable opening to any sentence.

Kate listened politely, the attentive smile on her lips concealing the pang the words cost her. It was foolish beyond reason to allow herself to fall in love. Serge had declared his intention of trying to seduce her and his loving words to her might only have been a means to an end. She would have to keep that thought constantly in her mind.

Yet she found herself dressing with care for the evening meal, putting on a low-necked gown of deep gold velvet that emphasised the shining flecks in her brown eyes. Looking at herself she wondered if

Aunt Natalya had been right to call her pretty. In her own eyes her nose was still too long and her mouth too wide but when she walked into the dining-room she saw Serge's eyes fixed upon her and felt suddenly beautiful.

'Did the funeral go well?' she asked, accepting a glass of wine from Peter.

'Quietly.' It was her uncle who answered. 'There are many who don't recall Father Fyodor at all, of course. You look festive tonight.'

There was an unspoken criticism in his tone and she thrust out her chin defiantly as she answered.

'I am celebrating my own rescue, Uncle Alexis. I am very sorry about the poor man but I didn't know him personally.'

'I think your dress is lovely,' Peter said. 'And you may be sure that I have excellent taste, but it seems a pity to waste it on an evening *en famille*. You ought to come back to St Petersburg with us. The season there is still at its height.'

If they did go they would stay overnight again at the monastery and this time she would seek out the priest and discover why her appearance had alarmed him so greatly.

'This is a business trip,' Serge said.

To Kate's disappointed surprise his face had become hard and cold again.

'Surely a few days in St Petersburg won't hurt,' Peter began.

'If Kate goes to the city then I shall go too,' Anna said in a shrill, tense little voice. She was leaning forward, her eyes stormy and her plump face flushed an unbecoming scarlet.

'You may go when you are married,' Aunt Natalya began.

'But I want to go now,' Anna said. 'I've been stuck in Narodnia since I was twelve years old, ever since my parents died, and I'm tired of never going anywhere, never meeting anyone.'

'Anna Nicholaevna! That sounds like ingratitude,' Aunt Natalya began.

'I'm sorry, I didn't mean to sound ungrateful,' the girl said in a sobbing breath. 'I love being here but I want to see more of life before I'm too old to enjoy it!'

She gave one piteous look around the circle of faces and went, stumbling over the hem of her frilled dress, out of the room.

'I will go and talk to her,' Aunt Natalya

began but Serge had risen, setting down his wine-glass with a little thump.

'The girl is my responsibility. I'll smooth her down,' he said, rising and following her out.

'It begins to look as if Serge is about to become more dutiful,' the Count said. 'We may see a wedding yet at Narodnia.'

Kate said nothing but her fingers tightened round the stem of her wine glass. Serge had gone out with real concern on his face and it hurt her to see it. Perhaps her uncle was right and after a flirtation with his English cousin he would act the dutiful son and marry his father's ward as the family expected him to do. The thought was an unbearable one.

'We may as well eat,' the Count said, rising and offering Kate his arm. 'Serge will coax Anna back into a good humour but I don't intend to go hungry while he's doing it!'

'And we shall make an early start tomorrow,' Peter said. 'I wish you were coming, Kate. We shall be away for about a week.'

'And I'm certain you will contrive to amuse yourself while you're in the city,' his aunt said, 'so let us hear no more about poor Kate's being dragged off on her travels again. I am just getting to know her and you want to deprive me of her company so soon.'

They were eating the fish when Serge returned, leading a somewhat chastened Anna by the hand. The girl's eyelids and the tip of her nose were pink, her demeanour sorrowfully penitent, but she shot a sullen glance at Kate from beneath her reddish lashes as she took her place at the table.

It was an uncomfortable meal that encapsulated all the uneasiness Kate had sensed in the house over the past two days. The house itself had welcomed her as if it had always been her home but there was someone in the house who wanted her gone. She could feel the rejection almost like a physical force pushing her out but she couldn't tell from whom it came.

After the meal Aunt Natalya took her seat at the pianoforte and, as if she were instinctively trying to cheer the atmosphere, played a variety of tinkling French tunes but the notes sounded forced and disjointed in the luxuriously appointed room.

Kate, glancing at Serge, wondered how it had been when her mother had been governess here. Aunt Natalya would have been a young girl, her hair in ringlets and her grandparents would have sat down here, Babushka tapping time to the music and her grandfather exchanging an occasional word with his gentle elder son. Had Anne Rye lifted her eyes from her needlework or her book to steal a glance at Boris and had he ever ventured to return it?

The gathering broke up early, the Count declaring that it was his intention to set off in good time.

'If we had delayed our return to Narodnia we could have settled this business of contracts. However, we'll make what speed we can on the journey. Are there are errands you ladies want in St Petersburg?'

'Nothing, Alexis dear,' Aunt Natalya stopped playing to say.

Kate said her own good nights and went up to her room. The uneasiness was still all around her and she was being swallowed up in it, the cool and independent Kate Rye becoming fearful and uncertain. She had put on her robe and was sitting by the fire when there was a tap on the door.

'Katinka, may I come in for a moment?' Serge asked.

'Yes, of course.' She frowned slightly as he entered, remembering his cold attitude towards her earlier that evening.

'We leave first thing for St Petersburg,' he said, 'so you'll still be abed when we set out. I came to bid you a more friendly good-night.'

'Oh?' She tried to speak coolly but he had bent to take her hands and she could feel her legs trembling.

'I intend to—' he began and paused, his expression curiously uncertain.

'Yes?' She looked up at him, her own face reflecting the conflict in his.

'Never mind. Take care of yourself in the time I'm away.'

He gave her fingers a brief, hard squeeze and went out again, leaving her staring after him in bewilderment.

ELEVEN

The uneasiness intensified after he had gone. When she finally went to bed she fell into a disturbed sleep, broken by faceless and threatening images that loomed over her and then withdrew. Once she half-woke, thinking she heard voices raised somewhere beyond the window but it was only the sound of the wind rising amid the pines and sweeping down across the plateau to the house.

It was broad daylight when she woke and for a moment she felt a surge of gladness because she was at Narodnia, in the house where her father had lived and fallen in love with her mother just as she was now falling in love with Serge.

The two little maidservants hadn't come. The water in the jug was cold and the fire had dropped into ashes. Kate splashed her face and put on her warm, dark dress, braiding her hair over her ears. She was just completing her toilet when Marisa entered with the breakfast tray.

'Mademoiselle, I apologise for the lateness,' she said, 'but there has been a contretemps and we are behindhand.'

'Why? What's happened? Is Babushka worse?' Kate asked sharply.

'No, no, Madame Ilsa is much improved but Mademoiselle Anna is not in her room,' the housekeeper said.

'Not in her room? Then where is she?' Kate asked.

'Mademoiselle Natalya will explain it to you. She is most distressed by the little one's conduct.'

'Do you mean she's run away?' Kate demanded. 'She said last evening she wished to go to St Petersburg.'

'I wish *you* had returned to the city,' Marisa said abruptly. 'I wish you had never come to Russia. You brought all the past back to us.'

'What part of the past?' Kate pushed away the breakfast tray, which was untouched, and faced the older woman challengingly. 'Ever since I arrived you've made it clear that I was unwelcome. You've let fall dark hints of danger and so has Babushka.'

'You would do well to heed,' Marisa said.

'To heed what?' Kate almost stamped her foot in exasperation. 'Oh, I'm not a complete fool. I know there's a secret connected with my father's death but I haven't found out yet what it is. I mean to find out whatever you say.'

'Mademoiselle, I beg of you to go no further,' Marisa said. Her normally pale face was chalky white and her voice shook with suppressed emotion.

'It has to do with Igor Kerinsky, hasn't it?' Kate pressed on. 'The servant who was hanged for theft? It began with him. Babushka thinks he was innocent.'

'Madame Ilsa is elderly and she gets confused.'

'Not so old and not always confused,' Kate flashed. 'You were here then, weren't you? You remember Igor Kerinsky. If he didn't take the jewels—'

'They were found sewn into his mattress in his room,' the other interrupted. 'There was no doubt of his guilt.'

'Who found them there?'

'The master conducted his own personal search. Igor was a trusted servant, one of the few with access to every room in the house. Mademoiselle, I urge you to go no further in the matter, to ask no more questions.'

'If you'll excuse me?' Kate spoke with teeth clenching politeness.

Marisa gave an eloquent shrug of the shoulders that was more Gallic than Russian and moved aside.

Aunt Natalya, a damp handkerchief balled in her hand, swung around as Kate entered the drawing-room and exclaimed:

'Has Marisa told you? I would not have believed it of them. All the while deceiving us and then to run off together in such a fashion!'

'She said Anna was not in her room.'

'Indeed Anna is not in her room,' Aunt Natalya said. 'She is on her way to St Petersburg to marry Peter according to the note she left pinned to her pillow. Peter set off ahead of the others, no doubt to catch up with her and provide escort. And Alexis and Serge had left by the time Anna's note was found.'

'Anna and Peter,' Kate said slowly.

The snatch of conversation she had overheard was clear to her now and Anna's jealousy understandable if she believed her sweetheart had been paying attention to the English newcomer.

'It's wrong,' Aunt Natalya said. 'It was to be Serge and Anna. I made up my mind to that and Alexis agreed with me.'

'But if she loves Peter, what's to be gained from preventing the marriage?' Kate asked in bewilderment.

'It is the duty of a young girl to obey her elders,' Aunt Natalya said obstinately. 'My dear father always impressed upon us that duty must come before self-gratification. I have lived my life according to that precept and it has never done me any harm.'

'Aunt Natalya, Serge doesn't love Anna. In fact, I've reason to think he may be falling in love with me,' Kate said. 'I know it will outrage all the conventions if we marry but you said yourself that some traditions are outworn.'

'You and Serge?' Aunt Natalya's face was a study. 'My dear, are you sure? Serge can be the most dreadful tease and both he and Peter are great flirts. I wouldn't want you to be hurt.'

'I think I'm sure,' Kate said.

'Then I have something to give you!' The other, her tears quenched, had arisen. 'Oh, I must confess that I did wonder if he might be attracted to you but last evening he seemed so cool that I decided I must be mistaken. So you and Serge are in love and Peter has eloped with Anna. It's like a fairy tale!'

'You're pleased then?'

'Pleased!' Aunt Natalya clasped her hands. 'Oh, my dear Kate, if you only knew! But come! I said I had something to give you. In a way it's a souvenir of your dear mother.'

She was bustling Kate out of the drawing-room and along the corridor to the chapel. On the threshold the girl hesitated for an instant, remembering the body that had recently lain there, but the vaulted chamber was cool and peaceful, the red lamp glowing near the smiling statue.

'Down here.' Aunt Natalya leaned within the shadowy alcove, fumbling at the wooden panels, letting out her breath in a little whistle of relief as one of the panels slid aside. 'Bring a candle with you. There are candles down here but they will require lighting and the steps are dark.'

The steps led steeply down into a wide, low-ceilinged corridor with stubs of candles placed in wide saucers on a shelf running down one side. Kate used the flame of the candle she was carrying to ignite their wicks, gazing in astonishment at the rocky walls with their surfaces scored with names and inscriptions in Russian characters.

'What is this place?' she asked.

'The old dungeons, I think. I suspect the first Narodny who built the house imprisoned disobedient serfs down here— political enemies too, to judge from some of the inscriptions. Those were barbaric times. I found this place by accident when I was a girl. Sometimes, if I was unhappy, I used to come down here, just to be quite alone and to sit peacefully.'

'It's a gloomy place,' Kate said.

'But private,' Aunt Natalya smiled, her gentle blue eyes moving reflectively about the rocky chamber. 'I used to come here with Igor, so for me it's always been a happy place.'

'Igor Kerinsky? The servant?'

'You said that in the way my father would have spoken the name, with a little flick of amused contempt,' her aunt said. 'No, I don't blame you! It was very undutiful of me to fall in love with a servant. My only excuse is that I was a very young girl, very foolish and romantic. Well, it wasn't to be! My dear father said that Igor had stolen some jewels that belonged to my mother and hidden them in his mattress intending to dispose of them later. He was hanged for it.'

'I think he was innocent,' Kate said. 'I think your father put the jewels there himself and laid the blame on Igor Kerinsky!'

'I think so too,' her aunt agreed. 'I know that Igor confessed to the theft but he had his family to consider. They might have been ruined if my father had decided to ruin them. He was a powerful and ruthless man. But I didn't bring you here to tell you old tales. I said I had a gift for you.'

She held out a sheet of rolled parchment tied with a length of red cord.

'What is it?' Kate took the roll and stared at her aunt.

'It's in Russian, so you'll not be able to read it,' the other said, 'but it's legal. A certificate of marriage between Anne Rye and my brother Boris. It seems that you are legitimate after all.'

'But how—where did you get this?' Kate asked.

'Father Fyodor conducted a secret marriage ceremony for Boris and your mother,' Aunt Natalya explained. 'She must have just suspected that she was pregnant, so they persuaded Father Fyodor to marry them, hoping to reconcile my father to the fact later on. But poor Boris died and Father Fyodor was in a blind panic lest his part in the affair come out, so he became a *starets* and took the marriage licence with him.'

'But he heard that the child of that marriage was here at Narodnia and so he came here to give me—' Kate's voice trailed away and she raised troubled eyes to the tiny, black-clad figure on the steps.

Aunt Natalya nodded, smiling.

'I met him first,' she said simply. 'He tried to run when he saw me but he was an old man and the ice was slippery and he fell. He was dead when I reached him and the snow was covering him fast, so I took the licence and left him for others to find.'

'And said nothing? But why not? And why give it to me now? Why?'

'Because I thought it only right that you should have the comfort of knowing your parents were legally wed.'

'My father—how did my father die?'

'Under the ice. He fell through the ice.'

'But was it an accident. Was it?' She didn't know what had impelled her to ask. She only knew that a cold horror was creeping through her.

'Boris saw me with Igor,' Aunt Natalya said. 'He was very shocked. I had shamed the family, you see, and it was his duty to tell father what had been going on. His *duty!* And all the time he was sleeping with my governess, with a nobody employed to teach me English! Igor was hanged for loving me and Boris was drowned for loving Anne Rye. Oh, it was very simple. I saw him on his way out to skate and I went out too, round to the other side of the lake, and called to him. I told myself that it was in the hands of God. He might not have fallen through where the ice was thin, or someone might have heard him call for help.'

'But you must have heard him!'

'I hid among the pine trees and listened to him,' Aunt Natalya said. 'He went under the water within a few seconds. I couldn't have saved him.'

'But you knew the ice was thin?'

'In the centre of the lake, yes. Boris was aware of it too but he was always dreamy and when he heard me calling I suppose that any thought of danger went out of his head. It was God's will.'

'And then Father Fyodor left?' Kate was in the grip of a living nightmare, trying to make sense of the events in her own mind.

'I suppose he feared that your mother would reveal the marriage in the hope of claiming something for her unborn child, so he left and took the proof with him.'

'And my mother left too, after Uncle Alexis's wife died. Why then?'

'Olga was a weak, foolish creature,' Aunt Natalya said impatiently. 'She was always ailing. No fit mother for those two little boys. I looked after them much more efficiently.'

'You killed her,' Kate said flatly.

'A little more medicine than was actually prescribed, a window opened for an hour while she lay asleep. It was God's will. Your mother had left by then and we were never able to trace her. I suppose she was afraid, suspecting me but never able to prove anything.'

'She intended to come back,' Kate said slowly. 'She made up her mind to return when I was a grown woman. At the monastery, on the way here, there was a priest who seemed to recognise me and told me to go away.'

'I suppose Father Fyodor mentioned his suspicions,' Aunt Natalya said. 'The monks would never have spoken out. They are dependent on our patronage.'

'Babushka guessed. She knows there is danger here.'

'Guesses but can never prove. Would you find it easy to suspect your own child?'

'And now?' Kate spoke warily but she sensed the answer.

'You will have to stay here,' her aunt said, gently regretful. 'Nobody will hear you even if you scream and bang and when the men return from St Petersburg I'll tell them you left. Nobody knows about these cellars except me.'

'I know about them, Mademoiselle,' Marisa said from the top of the stairs.

'But you'll not tell? You'll not say anything?' Aunt Natalya swung around, lifting her eyes pleadingly to the tall figure.

'The men didn't go to St Petersburg,' the housekeeper said. 'Oh, Peter and Anna have run away together, it's true, but the Count and Serge have returned. They plan to catch you in the act, Mademoiselle.'

'But it's God's will,' Aunt Natalya said, wringing her hands together. 'I have always done my duty, always been the instrument of God's will. Boris had to be punished for seducing my governess and Olga had to die so that I could look after her two motherless children.'

'And now it has to end,' Marisa said. 'We were never certain, Madame Ilsa and I, but since Mademoiselle Kate came, now we begin to see what has happened. It has to end. There must be no more deaths.'

'They should not have hanged Igor,' Aunt Natalya said.

She began to mount the steps, shaking her head a little, her voice sadly reflective as she moved past the housekeeper: 'They should not have hanged Igor.'

'I said you ought never to have come here,' Marisa observed, dislike in her eyes as she stared down at Kate. 'You brought back the past to her.'

'And uncovered murder. I can't think that's such a bad thing.'

Kate too mounted the stairs and stepped past the statue into the chapel.

'Igor was as good as murdered,' Marisa said. 'Hanged on a trumped-up charge because he dared to raise his eyes to the daughter of the house. You should have not come here, Mademoiselle.'

Kate turned away, aware of the futility of argument and went through to the hall. The front door was open and she glimpsed Aunt Natalya's small, black-gowned figure hurrying across the snow.

'You're safe!' The exclamation came from Serge who hurried down the passage towards her. 'Father and I began searching the house.'

'Marisa knew where to find me.' Kate spoke shiveringly.

'Come to the fire.' Serge put his arm around her and led her into the drawing-room, raising his voice to announce, 'She's here, Father, and no harm done.'

'Thank God for that!' Her uncle came forward, his expression sombre. 'I've not known what to think since Serge mentioned his suspicions to me but we hoped that our apparent departure to St Petersburg might precipitate events.'

'How long have you known?' Kate began in confusion.

'When you mentioned the priest having told you to go back I made enquiries at the monastery,' Serge said. 'He was reluctant to tell me anything but he admitted that Anne Rye had stayed at the monastery on her way back to England years ago. She had told him she was secretly married to Boris and fearful because she couldn't believe his death an accident. Oh, she hadn't known whom to suspect. She'd been concerned only with getting safely away.'

'And then your nearly burning yourself in your bed and getting lost in the blizzard,' her uncle continued. 'I began to think back to the time when Boris and then Olga died and Father Fyodor left so suddenly. It began to fit together, in a dreadful logical way.'

'Aunt Natalya had lost her chance of a husband and children,' Serge said. 'She wanted me to marry Anna but Anna and I hadn't the slightest interest in each other.'

'A pity,' his father put in, 'because it would have been an excellent match.'

'When you came she saw that I was interested in you,' Serge went on. 'I tried to put her off the scent by acting coolly towards you but she is too intelligent to be fooled. And that put her in a cleft stick. She knew you were legitimate and she could never tell. It must have been hard all these years for her to keep silent, knowing that Boris had been married to Anne Rye—'

'How did she know that?' Kate asked.

'If you please, Mademoiselle,' Marisa said from the door, 'she never was completely certain until Father Fyodor came and she took the marriage licence from him that Anne Rye gave him to keep for her. She always suspected but she was never sure.'

'She must be insane,' Kate said and shuddered.

'She was robbed of her love,' Marisa said. 'Fifteen years old and her sweetheart hanged. And it was Boris who told the master when all the time he'd secretly married the English governess.'

'She will have to be put under restraint,' the Count began unhappily.

'No, sir.' It was Marisa who spoke and there was authority in her dark eyes and quiet voice. 'No sir, to be confined would never suit Mademoiselle Natalya. It is more than twenty years since these events took place and at this lapse of time you could prove nothing. And the scandal would kill Madame Ilsa.'

'But something will have to be done,' Serge began impatiently.

'Yes, sir.'

Something in the housekeeper's tone

struck Kate and she said quickly:

'Where is Aunt Natalya now? I saw her going out!'

'Only for a short walk,' Marisa said, 'to the lake.'

'The lake?' Kate dropped the two words into a sudden silence.

'The surface is frozen but in places it's beginning to thaw,' Marisa said without expression. 'It's kinder to wait a little before we follow. Sometimes an accident can solve many problems.'

Kate wanted to protest, to run out and prevent whatever was happening, but Serge had taken her hands in his own warm clasp and his brilliant eyes held her own as he said:

'Marisa is right. This is the kindest way, Katinka. She must be given the grace of finding her own way out.'

'If I had never come,' she said unhappily, 'this would not have happened.'

Her uncle was going out into the hall with Marisa and for this little space of time she and Serge were alone in the big, firelit apartment.

'If I had never come,' she repeated unhappily, 'the past would have remained buried.'

'If you had never come,' he said, 'then you and I would have been cheated of our beginning.'

The shadows had not yet lifted but there was a promise in his words.

The publishers hope that this book has given you enjoyable reading. Large Print Books are especially designed to be as easy to see and hold as possible. If you wish a complete list of our books, please ask at your local library or write directly to: Dales Large Print Books, Long Preston, North Yorkshire, BD23 4ND, England.

This Large Print Book for the Partially sighted, who cannot read normal print, is published under the auspices of

THE ULVERSCROFT FOUNDATION

THE ULVERSCROFT FOUNDATION

. . . we hope that you have enjoyed this Large Print Book. Please think for a moment about those people who have worse eyesight problems than you . . . and are unable to even read or enjoy Large Print, without great difficulty.

You can help them by sending a donation, large or small to:

**The Ulverscroft Foundation,
1, The Green, Bradgate Road,
Anstey, Leicestershire, LE7 7FU,
England.**
or request a copy of our brochure for more details.

The Foundation will use all your help to assist those people who are handicapped by various sight problems and need special attention.

Thank you very much for your help.